This ~~plate~~ book belongs to ↘

(Excellent balancing)

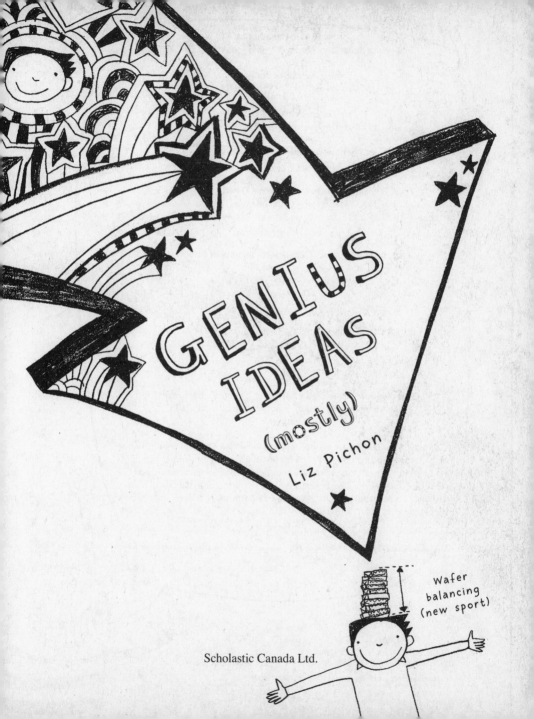

GENIUS IDEAS

(mostly)

Liz Pichon

Wafer balancing (new sport)

Scholastic Canada Ltd.

Scholastic Canada Ltd.
604 King Street West, Toronto, Ontario M5V 1E1, Canada

Scholastic Inc.
557 Broadway, New York, NY 10012, USA

Scholastic Australia Pty Limited
PO Box 579, Gosford, NSW 2250, Australia

Scholastic New Zealand Limited
Private Bag 94407, Botany, Manukau 2163, New Zealand

Scholastic Children's Books
Euston House, 24 Eversholt Street, London NW1 1DB, UK

www.scholastic.ca

Library and Archives Canada Cataloguing in Publication
Pichon, Liz, author
Genius ideas (mostly) / by L. Pichon.
(Tom Gates)
Originally published: London : Scholastic, 2012.
ISBN 978-1-4431-3303-6 (pbk.)
I. Title. II. Series: Pichon, Liz Tom Gates.
PZ7.P53Gen 2013   j823'.92   C2013-905487-1

Copyright © 2012 Liz Pichon.
First published in the UK by Scholastic Children's Books, 2012.
This edition published by Scholastic Canada Ltd., 2014.
All rights reserved.

6 5 4 3 2 1   Printed in Canada 116   14 15 16 17 18

To my sister

Lyn
xx ♡

Who made me EXCELLENT toys, bought lovely books and showed me how to draw with fancy pens and crayons.

Fancy crayons

Beddy Byes

(This card was a bit annoying, though)

THIS is a **GENIUS** idea... A FLIP BOOK in a book. Watch the bug dance

If my writing looks a bit "WOBBLY",

it's because I've just had a

TERRIBLE SHOCK!

So to help me calm

"" ""

down,

I'm searching 👁 👁 for the

SPECIAL

EMERGENCY
BISCUITS

I keep hidden under my bed.

(This is definitely an emergency.)

biscuit crumbs

PHEW! That's better.

OK, let me explain what happened. I was
in the bathroom, pretending to have a shower
while reading my comic (like you do).

When SOMEONE started **KNOCKING**
really **loudly** on the door.
I assumed it was my
sister Delia ...
... so I ignored her.

Then she did it again ...

... and again ...

... and again.

Knock

Knock

Knock Knock

The noise was **very** annoying. But I managed to carry on reading 👁 👁 EVERY single page of my comic **REALLY** slowly. **EVENTUALLY** when I'd finished, I very CAREFULLY opened the bathroom door. →

I was expecting Delia to SHOUT at me for

taking so long. I wasn't expecting to see **this.** ➡

It was a HORRIBLE Sight! I let out a LOUD

ARGH!

Which made Dad 🙂 come running out of the bedroom to see what all the **noise** was about. He said, "What's the problem here?" 😠 So I said, "Delia's the problem. She **l👓👓ks** **SCARY** without her 👓← sunglasses!"

Then Dad said it would be **nice** to have just ONE morning without being (disturbed) 😠 by the two of us **⚡ARGUING**.

Delia got REALLY CROSS and pointed at ME, ➡ saying I was the only one who was "DISTURBED". Then she told Dad that he looked

totally ridiculous.

Before disappearing into the bathroom and

slamming the door.

Which left me in

FULL VIEW ➡

of what Dad was wearing.

I couldn't decide who looked WORSE:

Delia without her sunglasses or Dad in his cycling shorts ? Mum wasn't much help either. She came upstairs and

SHOUTED, "Why is everyone shouting?"

Followed quickly by "And what on EARTH are you wearing?" Dad pointed out that she was the only one who was shouting and the cycling shorts were all part of his

Carefully planned new fitness regime.

Which made Mum LAUGH out loud.

ha! ha! ha!

I decided that this was probably a good time to head back to my room because:

NASTY SURPRISES + SHOCKS = EMERGENCY BISCUITS

It's a good job I keep a few hidden for these kinds of situations. I just hope there are no more unwanted surprises today. Sigh... I eat half of the (second) emergency wafer and start to imagine what MY idea of a FUN AND VERY RELAXING day at school would be. Mmmmmmm ... I think it would probably go something like this...

Mr Fullerman is DELIGHTED to see me (even though I'm late).

Hello, Tom, VERY good to see you.

I have my own special **COMFY** chair and table that are as ⟶ far away as possible from that very annoying **M**arcus **M**eldrew.

Marcus

sneaky snack box

far away

comfy chair

Lessons are OPTIONAL so I can choose what I want to do (which is easy).

Choose Your LESSONS Today	
ART	✗
MATHS	✓
Doodling	
MUSIC	✗
Spelling	
FUN Experiments	✓

Our NICE new art teacher Miss Straw insists I do a WHOLE art project on ...

CARAMEL WAFERS.

Really? If you insist

I have *f*u*n* arranging them into towers before spending as MUCH time as I want drawing and doodling. Miss Straw is VERY

Sigh

impressed

Well done, Tom!

and lets me eat TWO wafers for my snack. AND I'm allowed to unwrap the others and use the foil for my interesting wafer collage.

(13)

(The wafers I can save to eat later.)

Miss Straw thinks I am an ART BISCUIT GeNiuS.

I agree.

Well done, Tom.

What can I say? You deserve 100 merits for this AMAZING collage!

Miss Straw

(I show my 100 merits to Marcus, which annoys him.)

Then the day gets even better. A few friends and I have a DELICIOUS lunch served by ...

... the teachers.

More iced water, Tom?

TEACHERS' TABLE

I eat in the best part of the dinner hall (for a change). I'm allowed to have SECONDS of pudding, followed by a relaxing rest with my feet up before the next lesson starts.

Which is

EXTRA FUN EXPERIMENTS.

(Outside – because it would be SUNNY on my perfect day.)

The whole class helps me place hundreds of WAFERS in a long, row around the school. Then I get to PUSH the first wafer forward, causing them all to fall one by one in an AMAZING pattern (like dominoes).

Solid

Amy Porter

The SpecTAcuLAR

WAFER DISPLAY breaks the

WORLD BISCUiT FALLING RECORD! YEAH!

(And everyone gets to eat a few more of them too.)

Then as a **special** treat, **M**r Fullerman announces that our (MUSIC LESSON 🎵) today will be taught by ...

DUDE 3, only the **BEST BAND** EVER! Who arrive at our school in their fancy ↕ **HUGE**

tour bus. They put on a fantastic concert for the [entire] school, and because Derek (my best mate) 😊 and I are **DUDE 3**'s **BIGGEST** fans, we get to stand on stage and play along with our own guitars 🎸 😀 😀 to [all] the songs that we know. **DUDE 3** congratulate **US** on how good **WE** are. Which makes **M**arcus pull a face like this: 😕 (Huh?)

But that's NOTHING ...

compared to the LOOK on Delia's face

 when DUDE 3 pull up outside

OuR house in their tour bus.

Then me and Derek

get out, saying, Later, Dude3

to the whole band,

who wave back.

Then we carry our BRAND

NEW COOL guitars that the band have

given us back to the house.

Now THAT'S MY idea of the BEST and MOST AMAZING DAY at school EVER!

Oh well... You never know. Today might turn out to be a GOOD day after all? Like LAST WEEK in assembly (which I wasn't looking forward to), Mrs Nap asked everyone a question.

Who can tell me what month it is and what year?

Before I could put UP my hand to answer, Marcus Meldrew practically LEAPT off the floor, waving his arm around, so Mrs Nap would pick him. She did.

But the REALLY funny bit was when Mrs Nap asked Marcus to sit down and he accidentally said LOUDLY,

Yes, Mummy.

Then he couldn't understand why we were all LAUGHING so much. Mrs Nap had to say,

> I think you meant to say
> YES, Mrs Nap.

It was HILARIOUS! I laughed a LOT that day. Right NOW, though, if Mum and Dad see how late I am, I'll be in trouble. Although I'm not sure they'd notice. I can still hear Mum chuckling EVERY time she says the words fitness regime like it's the FUNNIEST joke she's EVER heard.

I'm not laughing because I know that:

There's a good chance that he could start turning up at my school, or WORSE STILL, my friends' houses, wearing something EVEN more embarrassing than those BRIGHT BLUE CYCLING SHORTS.

IF THAT'S POSSIBLE?

I slip downstairs and grab some breakfast and realize that I am <u>properly</u> late for school now. Mum is upstairs and still a bit busy.

I could go and ask her to write me a nice LATE NOTE to give to

ha!
ha!

(Mum being busy)

Mr Fullerman, which would probably stop me from getting into any trouble?

OK, TOM

But why bother when

it's SO much easier ...

... just to write ✎ one myself.

(A genius idea.)

Dear Mr Fullerman,

~~Poor~~ Tom has had a VERY nasty shock
this morning due to his ~~rotten stupid~~
sister scaring him. I'm very sorry he's
late for school. His sister has been
warned not to scare him again (or else).

Because of his SHOCK, Tom might find
it hard to concentrate on any tricky
maths today. Just letting you know.

Thank you,

Rita Gates

There, all done!
(Hopefully Mr Fullerman won't suspect anything dodgy about my note. I didn't mention Dad's shorts, as that would take too long to explain.)

Dad comes downstairs and starts doing some weird kinds of stretching moves. Mum is SHOUTING from upstairs to me:

Have you gone yet, Tom?

So I say BYE to Dad quickly and remind him I might be going to Norman's house for a band practice tonight. He says, "Norman's house isn't too far. How about I run over and collect you?" And I say,

"NO WAY!"

just that little bit too quickly in case he decides to turn up looking like ...

well, like that. ➡️

I tell him Derek's dad is coming to pick us up.

"All sorted, no need to worry, Dad."

Good thinking ...

phew!

Derek's not waiting outside: he's already left for school. So I set off with my SPECIAL LATE NOTE safely in my bag.

As I walk past the shop, I'm (thinking) maybe I could POP in for a small snack ? (Good idea.) It takes me a while to choose what to have.

But because I have a LATE NOTE, I'm hoping Mr Fullerman will read it and say, (That's all fine, Tom.) then let me off the hook.

And if he doesn't, at least I'll have my snack to eat.

Fingers crossed.

mmmmm?

FRUIT CHews

When I finally arrive at school, no one is around. It's REALLY quiet EVERYWHERE. Apart from Mrs Nap's classroom, where I can hear some odd noises wafting out of her slightly open door.

It sounds a bit like ... CATS YOWLING IN PAIN.

Owww {w} ww

Awwwwww

I go and take a sneaky 👁 👁 peek
to see what's going on.
It is Mrs Nap.
She seems to be Singing
the WHOLE register?

Worse than that, Mrs Nap is making
the class sing their names back to her.
One by one. Which is PAINFUL
to hear.

Charlie Smith?

Charlie Smith
is here,
Mrs Nap.

Mrs Nap is being her usual
cheerful self when she sings.

"Isn't this FUN, everyone?"

And Charlie Smith (who's just sung his name) sings back, "NOOOOO, not really."

Which makes Mrs Nap a bit CROSS.
So she sings, "Oh dear ... let's sing it again from the beginning and this time we'll ALL do it properly."

Charlie Smith tries to sing, "I was only joking, Mrs Nap!"
But it's too late.

Luckily for me (and my class) Mr Fullerman doesn't do "register singing". I think we'd be there ALL day if he did.

I'm SO busy peering in the classroom that I don't hear Mrs Mumble behind me until she says,

Hello, Tom.

Which makes me JUMP.

"Shouldn't you be in class?"

I explain I was on the way there and I have a LATE NOTE. Mrs Mumble remembers there's a "special buddy talk this morning. Mr Fullerman was taking your class to meet some of the younger children."

So I say, "Great."

And I'm about to go off and find them.

Then she adds, "But I'm not sure WHICH class they've gone to. Best you wait in the school office with me until they're back so I can mark ✓ you in the register. We don't want you just wandering round school, do we?"

(Me wandering)

I'm thinking...

1. What **IS** a "buddy talk"?

2. How long will I have to sit in the school office for, as it can be a *BIT* awkward?

What are you doing here, Tom?

Mrs Mumble points to a seat and asks me
not to talk while she makes an announcement
over the loudspeaker.
At least this should be
fun to watch.

Mrs Mumble clears her throat
and LEANS into the speaker
while pushing a special RED button.
As soon as she starts speaking, her voice
goes all, well ...

Mumbly.

"**Attention**, OAKFIELD School, can I remind EVERYONE that this Friday it's **Teacher Training** Day, so school will be finished **ONE** **HOUR** earlier than usual."

I can just about hear **CHeers** coming from all over the school (which is funny).

"This lunchtime's chess club is cancelled due to an **EXTRA** rehearsal for Dancing Through the Decades with Mrs Nap."

Another slightly smaller **CHeer** goes around.

Then she finishes by telling everyone...

"One more thing. When Mr Fullerman returns to his class, could he send someone to collect **TOM GATES** from the school office, as he was **LATE** for school and is waiting in the office to be **COLLECTED**. Thank you."

huh?

GREAT, now the **WHOLE** school knows I'm late. **AND** Mrs Mumble has made me sound like I'm some kind of **PARCEL**.

(Groan.)

TOM GATES
(For collection)
THIS WAY UP

As Mrs Mumble's finished her message, I **MUST** remind her about my *LATE NOTE* so I don't get into trouble.

I say, "Mrs Mumble, I know I'm **LATE** but I have a *NOTE* to explain why."

And she says,

"That's good, Tom. I'd like to SEE that note."

Which makes me **PANIC** a bit.

My note is stuffed into my bag and I can't find it **anywhere.**

I put my bag down onto her desk so I can

have a good rummage around.

While I'm looking, I carefully explain

ALL about my OLDER sister Delia

and how she gave me a NASTY SHOCK

this morning (which is true, she did). But I

don't say what happened. Instead I recreate

my "I'M SHOCKED!" face like this...

Which startles

Mrs Mumble a bit.

And because I STILL

can't find my note, I

carry on...

"It's in here somewhere."
Then I tell Mrs Mumble how Mum
was a bit worried about me
because I looked slightly PALE.

"Mum told me I was CLAMMY
from the SHOCK and I needed to sit down
and recover a bit before going to school.
Which is why I'm late, Mrs Mumble."
I do a slightly different type of face ... like
this... ➡

Then breathe ☰3 a SIGH of relief,
as I've just found my note. I give it to Mrs
Mumble, who's about to read
it when there's a
KNOCK at the office door.

LATE note

Hello!

It's **AMY PORTER** from my class. She tells Mrs Mumble TWO things.

1. I can come back to class, as Mr Fullerman is there now.

I'm back.

2. The **WHOLE** school have just heard my (why I'm LATE) explanation because the

LOUDSPEAKER is still on.

IT IS?

M rs M umble LIFTS my bag off the SPECIAL red button and says,

"Oh dear, that'll be why."

I'm doing a "VERY embarrassed"

face, which looks like this...

Shame

Groan.

And if **that's** not bad enough, Mrs Mumble

only goes and brings out her

She says, "That reminds CAMERA.

me, Tom – I need a picture of you."

I say, "RIGHT NOW?"

Because I can feel my face going even

REDDER!

Mrs Mumble tells me that it's for the

school NEWSLETTER.

"You have a SPECIAL MENTION

for the EXCELLENT DRAWING HOMEWORK*

on your school book. Nothing to be

embarrassed about, Tom!"

*See page 357, Everything's Amazing (Sort Of).

Which **cheers** me up a bit. **I**'d forgotten about being in the NEWSLETTER.

At least **AMY** will see that I don't make stupid mistakes like this *all* the time. Speaking of stupid mistakes...

Mrs **M**umble is just about to take the photo when someone else **knocks**

at the door. There's a kid standing outside with a COMB ... ... STUCK in his **hair**.

Mrs Mumble looks at him and says, "How did you do that?"

The kid says he's not really sure.

Mrs Mumble tells him to Wait there, then goes ahead and takes what I hope will be a VERY Nice picture of me for the NEWSLETTER.

SMILE

Now Mrs Mumble's got this kid with a comb stuck in his hair to deal with, my LATE NOTE seems to have ⟩slipped her notice, which is a

BIG RELIEF.

Phew

On the way back to class, AMY PORTER wants to know exactly what Delia did that gave me such a ²SHOCK¹. I can't say "She took off her sunglasses, it was terrible" because that doesn't sound shocking at all. (Even though it was.)

Instead I say, "It was nothing, I'm over it now." (Like I'm being brave.)

Then I manage to quickly change the subject by asking AMY what the BUDDY TALK was all about. AMY says the YOUNGER kids get to choose an older kid (one of us) to be their BUDDY. ☺

"We have to look out for them and make sure they're happy in school. That kind of thing. Mr Fullerman took us to say hello so the little kids know who we all are now." I say, "Lucky them."

Since I wasn't there, I ask **AMY** what happens if you don't get chosen to be a buddy. **AMY** tells me,

"Not <u>all</u> the little kids want to have buddies. So don't worry, it will be less hassle for you not to be picked."

But I think I'd make a good **BUDDY**. I could show them all kinds of really **important** stuff, like:

○ How to be **first** in the lunch queue.

sneaky short cuts

Oh yes!

- How to get **BIG** portions of the food you like.

- How to get small portions of the food you don't like.

- Which teachers to look out for.

- Why **DUDE 3** are the **BEST BAND** in the whole world ...

Back in class, Mr Fullerman says,

Better late than NEVER, Tom.

I don't have to explain where I've been because everyone has already heard. (Groan.)

Marcus Meldrew can't WAIT to tell me how STUPID I sounded over the loudspeaker.

You sounded stupid

So I tell him,

"You don't need a LOUDSPEAKER to SOUND STUPID."

And he says, "No one will pick you as a buddy because you weren't there."

So I (think) quickly and say,
"No one will pick **YOU** as a buddy
because you WERE there."

Then Mr Fullerman GLARES at
both of us and says,

 STOP TALKING.

Which shuts Marcus up ... for now.

Mr Fullerman says today he's going to
read us a story. (I'm hoping this means
we'll have a nice RELAXing

day after all?)

Then he adds...

"**Listen** carefully, as we'll be doing some work about the story later."

(Groan...)

Mr Fullerman holds up a book and asks if anyone has heard of

Aesop's Fables?

And Mark Clump, who hardly EVER puts his hand up, gets VERY EXCITED and says,

Mr Fullerman, I HAVE, I HAVE. They're my favourite. ☺

Mr Fullerman asks Mark,

Which is your FAVOURITE FABLE, Mark?

And Mark Clump thinks for a while...
(Quite a long while, actually.)
Mr Fullerman looks impressed that Mark is thinking about his answer SO carefully.

Until he says...

Plain if it's toasted with butter

and jam ... yum.

Which isn't quite the answer
Mr Fullerman was expecting.

The class start LAUGHING Ha! Ha! Ha! Ha! Ha!

because we've just realized Mark thinks

Mr Fullerman said BAGEL.

Whoops

So just to make it clear for everyone,

Mr Fullerman says,

> # The FABLE –
> ## NOT BAGEL, FABLE –
> ## I'll be reading is called
> ## "THE BOY WHO CRIED WOLF".

Marcus nudges me and says he knows this

story already.

> ## The wolf eats the boy in the
> ## end ... that's it, really.

Thanks for telling me the

ending, Marcus.

That's just great.

The **good** news is **M**arcus has given me 🙂 an idea 💡 for a doodle. I carefully arrange a few innocent-looking books on my desk.

While **M**r **F**ullerman is reading out the story, I get busy drawing.

AMY is watching 🙂 and smiling. I have to keep stopping to pay attention to **M**r **F**ullerman.

(Me paying attention.)

Marcus has been ignoring me. **Until** right at the end of my drawing, when I do a 😐 picture of him ...

... that catches his eye.

Marcus has only gone and put his

hand UP and interrupted

Mr Fullerman, who's not very happy.

He tells Mr Fullerman,

"Sir! Tom Gates

is drawing, SIR."

Luckily for me, Mr Fullerman doesn't tell

me off. I just have to put down my pen

and LISTEN.

Which I do (for a while).

But **M**arcus is **still** watching me.
Which is annoying.

So I start to draw this line

Hey!
Marcus ➡ Yes, **YOU.** Follow this line

Don't stop looking!

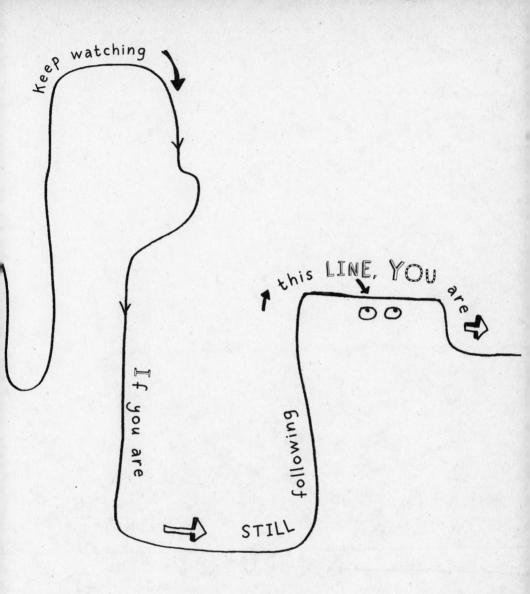

keep watching

this LINE, YOU are

If you are

following

STILL

AN IDIOT!

Ha!
Ha!
Ha!
Ha!
Ha!

64

Marcus looks like this now.

(I should try this trick
on Delia too!)

My best mate Derek ➡ 😊 🎵🎸 comes to find me. He can't come to band practice tonight, which is a shame.

😒 "I have to go to Aunt Julia's house with my mum." Derek looks really fed up.
"I hope she doesn't do that face-**squeeze** thing on me again.
It's embarrassing."

"Look at you!"
— Aunt Julia

To make Derek feel better, I tell him about when my Aunty Alice, 👓 Uncle Kevin 😊 and the cousins 😊 😊 came round for a family barbecue last weekend.

Derek says, "I **LOVE** barbecues."

And I say, "So do I, usually."

I explain to Derek,

"It would have been OK, but Dad

was in a REALLY BAD mood, mostly

because of Uncle Kevin and his dodgy jokes.

Eating for two?

AND he didn't like my

paper banger either, or the

noise it made. Then when Dad

dropped all the sausages on the

ground, he said it was MY fault!"

Derek says, "I was wondering where Rooster got those sausages from. And what's a paper banger*?"

I still have a paper banger **Scrunched** up in my pocket. So I take it out and try and smooth out the creases to make it work better. It's not great, but it does the trick.

I tell Derek, "I was only showing the cousins how to make it go **BANG!**

Like this ... by flicking it over my head..." **BANG**

*See page 308 on how to make a paper banger.

$\mathbb{D}$erek seems to have cheered up a bit and wants to have a go at making the paper banger work himself.

It takes a few tries,

duff

but eventually Derek gets it at the right angle

Bang!

... to make a very loud

BANG!

The noise attracts a bit of attention from some of the little kids in school, who come over and want to know

What's that?

"It's a paper banger," I tell them. "Look."

Then I show them how it works.

"You can make them yourself, it's easy."

BANG!

This kid called **Joey** wants to take a closer look. He's the one I saw in the school office with the comb stuck in his hair (which is out now).

I'm very nice and let **Joey** have a go. I show him the knack of making the banger work properly too. **W**hich is a mistake...

BANG!

He manages to **TEAR ALL** the paper up the sides. Joey says sorry and hands it back to me. It's just as well they're easy to make, because this one's ruined.

Whoops

Derek says **Joey** reminds him of **N**orman when he breaks stuff. **M**ind you, ever since **N**orman fell off his bike* and hurt his ⟵ elbows, he's been a bit more careful about everything he does.

Mind that banana skin.

Derek reminds me to tell Norman that we'll have to cancel band practice tonight. He suggests, "We could do it at the weekend instead?" **A**nd then he says **AGAIN**, "You won't forget to tell Norman, will you, Tom?" And I say, As if!

* See page 247 of Everything's Amazing (Sort Of) for the full story.

PE

(Stands for Physical Education, or in Norman's case, Poorly Elbows.)

Even though Norman is the FIRST person I see when I come into class, I completely forget to tell him about band practice. Norman gets to miss PE because of his elbows.

I ask him if he's being allowed to relax for a bit or do something else? Norman points to some worksheets and tells me, "Mr Fullerman wants me to catch up with these. He says the class have done them already."

We have? I take a quick look, but I don't remember doing **ANY** of these worksheets? I'll keep quiet and won't mention it in case Mr Fullerman wants me to catch up as well.

Tom!

Norman has to go and sit in the **school office** with Mrs Mumble

Ready, Norman?

(Groan.)

(like I did), while the rest of class 5F follow Mr Fullerman for PE.

Follow me!

We get changed and go outside to the playing fields, as the weather is nice and **WARM.**

Mr Fullerman announces to the class that we're about to have

LOTS of FUN!

And we all cheer! "YEAHHH!"

Then he adds,

Training for our SPORTS DAY!

Which makes us go...
"Awwwwwwwwwww."

 Training doesn't sound like much fun to me?

Mr Fullerman tells us to **Warm Up**

by running round the field ⇨ once.

Solid (who's not keen on running)
puts up his hand and says,
"Mr Fullerman, I am really
WARM already, so do I
have to run?"

I think Solid has made a
VERY good point.

So I say, "Sir, I'm VERY WARM too. Phew!..."

In the hope Mr Fullerman might change his mind about making us do all that running.

NO chance.

Mr Fullerman says,

TWICE round the playing fields for EVERYONE.

Ignoring both of us.

The whole class are GROANING now and staring at us. Apart from Brad Galloway, who loves running. Yes!

Florence Mitchell's not happy.

She says,

Nice work, Tom.

Whoops...

Like it's ALL MY FAULT!

Mr Fullerman is keeping his BEADY EYES on ME the WHOLE time I'm running.

I can't even hide behind a TREE or pretend to be doing up my shoelaces for a quick REST without him shouting,

"Keep going, TOM ... I can SEE YOU!"

I'm REALLY HOT and I've gone BRIGHT RED now.

 Solid can hardly SPEAK he's

SO PUFFED out.

He (just about) says,

"We've ... hardly ... started ... yet."

Which is true. (Groan.)

Marcus Meldrew comes over to ME and starts WaVing his hands around my head. (Which is annoying.) :(

I say, "What are you doing, Marcus?"

And he says,

"**M**y hands are **COLD**, I'm just warming them up ...

ON YOUR FACE!"

Ha!

HA!

Ha!

HA!

Marcus thinks he's **HILARIOUS.**

I think it's going to be a VERY **long** **PE** lesson.

Groan.

My class, 5F, have **never** (I repeat) **NEVER** won **ANYTHING** on SPORTS DAY. We're a bit rubbish compared 😔 to some of the other classes.

Every year at the end of SPORTS DAY Mr Fullerman says,

"WELL DONE, Class 5F, you've ALL done SO WELL! Just remember, it's the taking part that counts."

(Even though we've come last.)

While Mr Sprocket's class, Class 5S, are usually

✶ ★ **Celebrating** ⭐ ✶ ...

by WHOOPING and CHEERING

because they have won

SPORTS DAY AGAIN.

SPORTS DAY

Go Class 5S!

(Mr Sprocket doing his VICTORY ROBOT DANCE.)

85

Right now, from the way Mr Fullerman is making us do STAR ⭐ JUMPS

and bunny hops

(which are hurting my legs), I think he's hoping that THIS time SPORTS DAY could be a bit different for EVERYONE.

At LAST!

Sometimes I wonder why SPORTS DAY is actually called SPORTS DAY. I'm not sure EVERYTHING we do is a REAL sport?

Like...

Hula Hooping

Which is a LOT harder than it looks.

Skipping

Mr Fullerman says boxers skip to keep fit.
But they probably don't have someone like
Marcus standing RIGHT NEXT to them messing
up THEIR skipping
ROPE all the time.

Beanbag juggling

BEANBAGS get used a LOT on SPORTS DAY:

we do loads of throwing and catching

and running in between them.

My personal favourite is beanbag balancing.
It's fun to put them on your arms,
knees, or do a double balance on your
knee and
foot at the same time. I often pile them on my
head. Mr Fullerman tells me to
stop when I get to about here.

The LONG jump is the only "sport" we do today that I've seen 👁 👁 on telly. Mr Fullerman wants all of us to have a go. He tells us,

"You need a good *run* up, then throw your legs forward and jump into the sandpit."

Marcus starts bending his legs up and down. I say, "What are you doing, Marcus?" and he says, "I'm getting ready to do a VERY BIG jump, because I am really good at long jump." Now he's taking deep breaths as well (which is a bit odd).

Solid says to me, "Maybe he is good at long jump after all?"

I say, "Let's see."

We watch Marcus as he starts to **RUN** as fast as he possibly can toward the sandpit...

Then he LEAPS into the air and does a really really ...

... small jump.

Mr Fullerman says,

Good try, Marcus. Stretch your legs out next time.

Now Marcus thinks he's done a

BRILLIANT jump.

(He hasn't.)

Mr Fullerman finishes off our training session with what he says is a **WARM** DOWN.

Solid says the warm down is making him even **HOTTER.**

On the way back to school, I can hear Marcus telling ANYONE who'll listen that <u>he is</u> a natural at long jump. (He's not.)

Brad Galloway is doing that funny thing when you walk behind someone really closely and they don't know you're there. He's right behind Solid, copying everything he does. Solid doesn't notice for ages, until I tell him. He says, Good joke, Brad and wants to try it on someone else now.

Trouble is, Solid's a bit **TALL** and

noisy and his shadow keeps giving him away.

I know you're there, Solid.

Hello, Solid.

When we get back to school, Mr Fullerman asks us to help put away the "sports equipment" (I think he means the beanbags, hula hoops and skipping ropes 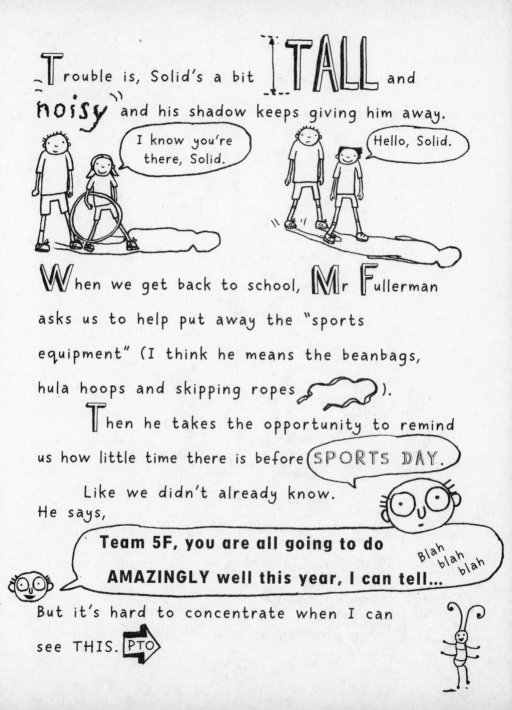).

Then he takes the opportunity to remind us how little time there is before SPORTS DAY.

Like we didn't already know.
He says,

Team 5F, you are all going to do AMAZINGLY well this year, I can tell...

Blah blah blah

But it's hard to concentrate when I can see THIS. PTO

Brad is going crazy behind Mr Fullerman's back.

I'm trying not to laugh, but it's almost impossible! Everyone who can see Brad dancing starts laughing too. Mr Fullerman gets a bit cross and says,

"This is NO laughing matter, Class 5F!"

Because he can sense something is going on behind his back. Then Mr Fullerman spins round SUPER FAST, just in time to catch Brad Galloway ...

... doing absolutely **nothing**.

(Lucky escape or what?)

Mr Fullerman says, "I'll be keeping a close **eye** on **YOU**, Brad."

Which is excellent news for ME, because (in between doing some work) I've been trying to finish my SUPER LARGE doodle in class.

Which is tricky to do with Mr Fullerman STARING at me (like he does).

I can't **WAIT** until lunchtime to catch up with Norman and Derek and tell them **ALL** about how **BRAD** was dancing behind **Mr Fullerman's** back.

In the dinner hall, I stand up to show them EXACTLY what he did. Like this:

" I am very busy **WAFTING** my arms around over my head and from side to *side*, recreating Brad's dance. I don't even **NOTICE** that DEREK is making a funny face at me. ⇨

I carry on and say, "Trust me ... it was **REALLY** funny! Especially when **Mr Fullerman** was going **ON** and **ON** about SPORTS DAY

and Brad Galloway was wobbling

his legs about like this..."

Then I tell them that the **BEST**

part of all was that

Mr Fullerman had ABSOLUTELY NO idea

what Brad was doing behind his back.

Derek nudges me and says...

"I think he does now."

Because Mr Fullerman is l○̇○̇king over in MY direction with his BEADY eyes and shaking his head in a very STERN and disapproving way. I have a horrible feeling that he's heard everything I've just said.

It's easy to forget about Mr Fullerman's SUPERHUMAN HEARING.

I should have known better. (It's happened to me before.)

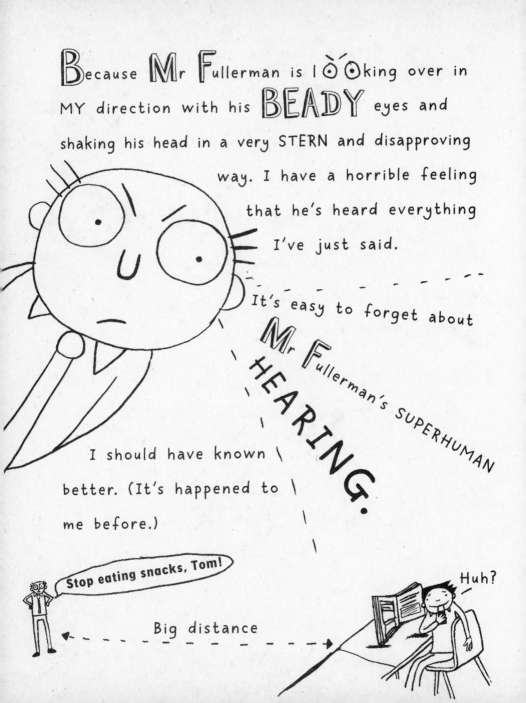

Stop eating snacks, Tom!

Huh?

Big distance

Norman says, "He's still looking."

I try and focus REALLY hard on my lunch and whisper,

"Tell me when he's stopped."

Then `two` VERY important questions suddenly POP into my head.

Question 1. Will Brad get into trouble because of me?

Question 2. Are those REALLY chips on top of my cake?

Answer 1. Mmmmm, possibly?

Answer 2. Yes, they are really chips because Granny Mavis has been cooking again.

I manage to carefully pick out the chips and eat the cake (the two don't usually go together unless you're Granny Mavis). Norman seems keen to eat my chips, which is fine by me (but a bit weird).

Yum

Then while he's eating, I ask Norman what it was like missing PE and having to do his work in the school office. And he says it was all right. But he did find out something interesting. And Derek and I both say,

WHAT'S that?

Norman tells us that he overheard a conversation in Mr Keen's office with Mrs Mumble.

Chips

He says, "They were both talking about BANDS."

"Really?"

Norman carries on, "I was being very quiet and not moving around much so I could listen. I heard Mr Keen say,

Norman NOT moving

"If we can get DUDE 3 to play for the school, that would be GREAT. The children would enjoy seeing them."

And I say,

"Are you sure?" And Norman says with a mouthful of chips,

Yes, I'm sure.

Derek wonders why DUDE 3 would want to play at OUR school? If it DOES turn out that DUDE 3 are playing in our school, that would be...

BRILL

AMAZ

FANTAST

Derek warns me that I shouldn't get TOO

"I mean, Norman's not totally sure Mr Keen

said DUDE 3 . He might have got it wrong.

No offence, Norman," Derek adds.

"None taken," Norman says.

But it's true. Norman does get stuff muddled

up sometimes.

Oh?

I said bring a
PEN,
Norman.

TOY HEN

We're getting ready to leave the dinner hall when we hear a MASSIVE

CRASH!

It's a BIG vegetable accident with a WHOLE tray of PEAS being spilled all over the floor.

We're trying to see exactly what happened.

Looks like it was that kid Joey (the one who broke my paper banger).

He's accidentally BUMPED into someone who was carrying the peas.

I can hear Caretaker Stan's keys jingling in the distance already, as he dashes to the dinner hall ...

squashed peas

... with a SUPER large BROOM

to get the peas under control.

(Which is proving very difficult to do.)

We leave Stan swishing his broom around with

a LONG trail of squashed peas behind us.

Mr Fullerman asks everyone
to **STAND UP** -

THEN **SIT DOWN** -

then **STAND UP** again and check under their

shoes for "squashed peas".

(This is another sneaky way of making us

practice for SPORTS DAY.)

AMY checks her shoes (which are clean).

Marcus has pea-free shoes as well. But

mine are COVERED in peas.

Marcus says it looks like I squashed a frog

and then he makes a
big deal of moving
his chair right away from me. Mr Fullerman
hands me a few paper towels, which
get rid of the peas nicely.

Marcus keeps saying YUCK! and pulling
horrible faces.

So I tell Marcus that he's got something
GREEN stuck between his
teeth that doesn't look so
good either. He hasn't ,
but it shuts him up for a bit.
Mr Fullerman wants Marcus to
MOVE his chair BACK to where ←
it was. And stop being so silly.
I agree...

Here's my doodle of Marcus inspired by peas.

(Marcus pea brain)

ENGLISH

Eventually we get the **S**quashed
peas under control, and **M**r **F**ullerman hands

out **TWO** WORKSHEETS while

making us do some extra arm

stretches at the same time.

Stretch up!

He says everyone can

choose which worksheet to

do. Then he STARES at Brad and says,

**"Brad, you might like to do worksheet one?
And don't forget, I do have eyes in the
back of my head."**

Which sounds like an odd thing

for **M**r **F**ullerman to say. **STOP
pulling
faces,
Brad**

Until I read worksheet one. (Brad's been

rumbled.)

Creative Writing Project 1

Read the beginning of this story carefully.
Then I'd like YOU to continue the story on
a separate piece of paper. Please write at
least one A4 page.

It was clear to Mr Fullerman that
SOMETHING was going on behind his
back. He decided the only thing to do
was ...

go home.

The end.

If I were
going to
write an
ending
for the
story on
worksheet
one, I'd
do this...
Ha! Ha!

Bit short, I know. Better do worksheet two instead

if I don't want to get into trouble (again).

Creative Writing Project 2

I would like you to write your own fable with a similar theme to the fable we read in class, "The Boy Who Cried Wolf". The story can be from your own imagination or based on something that might have happened to you in your own life.

At least one A4 page, please.

This is my version of a FABLE — all based on the family barbecue I was telling Derek about earlier that we had last weekend. Enjoy.

The Boy Who Said,

The Sausages Are Burnt

By Tom Gates

This is the story of a family who wouldn't listen to their **VERY** smart son ➡️ (that will be me, then). It all began when the ☀️**SUN** came out and my dad 🤠 thought it would be an **EXCELLENT** idea to have a barbecue. I said,

Doesn't it always rain when you get out the barbecue, Dad?

And he said,

Don't be **daft**, of course it's **NOT** going to rain!

(Like *THAT'S* never happened before.)

So I watched Dad wheel the barbecue out
from the corner of the garden.

It was covered with some special protective plastic that Dad told me would keep it

EXTRA clean and ready to use in an instant!

But underneath the "protective plastic" the barbecue was full of revolting **gunge**.

I told Dad the barbecue didn't look THAT clean? And Dad said that it just needed a quick brush down and all that BLACK **gunge** would **BURN** off during cooking.

I said,

Are you sure? It looks really disgusting.

But Dad wasn't listening to me. He was looking at Mum, who was *RUNNING* toward us in a very **BIG PANIC** She told Dad,

I've **COMPLETELY** forgotten that Uncle Kevin and Aunty Alice and the cousins are coming to lunch...

Dad said, **When?** And Mum said, **TODAY...** Which would have been OK until she added... **In five minutes!** Dad said, "Oh great." (But not in a *JOLLY* way.) Mum wanted to know how long the barbecue would take? And I said, "It will take FOREVER, it always does."

But Dad said, Don't listen to Tom.

And gave me a LOOK.

He ASSURED Mum that he knew EXACTLY

what he was doing. "I can just throw on a

couple of extra sausages for them."

← Extra
sausages

(Without wanting to SPOIL the story,

you can probably see what's happening here.)

 + NOT listening to me ⟹ = DISASTER

Dad

When Uncle Kevin arrived EARLY,

Dad was busy telling Mum that EVERYTHING

would be fine because he was a

barbecue expert. ☺

And Uncle Kevin said,

HELLO! Did someone say barbecue expert? I'm here!

 And Dad whispered, "Great, that's all I need." So Mum suggested that we should leave both the barbecue experts to get on with **burning** the lunch.

Which Dad didn't think was very funny.

All this talk of sausages was making me hungry. I really HOPED the barbecue wasn't going to take too long.

Aunty Alice and the cousins were in the kitchen holding a MASSIVE bag of snacks. I told them they should

EAT them NOW

because the barbecue could take AGES. Aunty Alice looked SURPRISED and said,

You're having a barbecue? I thought it was going to rain.

Mum said it would all be fine. (It wouldn't.) Then she asked me to go up stairs and let Delia know that everyone was here. And I said,

What's the point, she won't be pleased to see us.

Which was true.

Mum said, "Just go and knock on her door."

But **I** had a **MUCH** better idea than that.

I showed the cousins how to make some **paper bangers** and

how to use them too.

Then we all took them upstairs and stood outside Delia's bedroom door. I think using the paper bangers to let Delia know that everyone was here was a **genius idea!**

We flicked them over our heads, again ...

... and AGAIN...

BANG!

... and AGAIN...

BANG!

... and AGAIN...

Bang!

... and AGAIN...

Bang!

(That was a good one!)

Delia came **storming out** of her room and told us to **STOP** being annoying little boys.

So I told Delia that the cousins were NOT little and she was being rude.

Before Delia could get even more grumpy, Mum called upstairs and told us,

The barbecue is nearly ready!

I lOOked out into the garden but all I could see was

Thick SMOKE EVERYwhere.

The smoke seemed to be getting THiCKeR and thicker. Mum had to rush round the whole house closing the windows to stop the SMOKe from coming in. I couldn't see Dad at all. I could only hear him calling from the smoke-filled garden for someone to...

Bring me a PLATE QUICKLY!

Turns out Uncle Kevin wasn't much help after all. He'd escaped back to the house because he said the smoke was getting in his eyes and he couldn't stop coughing.

cough

coug

Mum handed me a plate to give to Dad (which I did).

Eventually when the smoke died down, I could see that the sausages all looked a bit ...

OVERDONE?

Dad said it was important for barbecued meat to be cooked properly and I shouldn't worry.

They're fine.

I watched Dad turn the meat over and cook them a bit more. I'd never seen sausages that colour before. I asked Dad if the barbecue was ready yet.

And he said, **NEARLY.**

And I said, "The sausages look a bit ... **burnt**, Dad?"

And Dad said "They're not burnt, they're just WELL DONE."

But when he tried to take the sausages off the barbecue and put them on the plate, they were ALL **stuck fast** to the nasty black **gunge** left on the grill. I reminded Dad that he said the **gunge** would burn off during cooking. And Dad told me I should go back to the house and find something more USEFUL to do.

Tell everyone that lunch is all under control.

(It wasn't.)

I left Dad scraping the sausages up while trying not to make too much of a mess on the plate.

Mum was trying to keep the smoke out of the kitchen with lots of tea-towel wafting. She asked me how everything was going.

I said, OK ... sort of. Which wasn't EXACTLY what Mum wanted to hear.

The cousins had taken my advice and eaten all the snacks.

Empty

SNACKS

Now they were playing with their paper bangers again.

BANG

BANG

I joined in and discovered that if I timed my paper banger SWING just right ...

NOISE

I couldn't hear a word Mum was saying.

"Sorry, Mum?"

BANG!

At least it took my mind off the burnt barbecue lunch that I knew was coming.

FINALLY Dad appeared through the SWIRLING smoke that was still hanging around

looking very pleased with himself and holding a nice BIG plate of (**burnt**) barbecued food. Well, he WAS holding a plate ... right up until I SWISHED the paper banger over my head and made a SPECTACULARLY LOUD...

BANG!

Dad was SO STARTLED

he tripped ...

... which fell on the ground ... and let go of the plate ... along with all the food ...

... that got covered

in grass ... and loads of ants.

(Extreme close-up)

Yeah!

sausages

(Who were attracted by the black sticky gunge.)

And just when Dad thought that this barbecue couldn't possibly get any worse, it started to RAIN.

A lot.

Uncle Kevin's eyes got better just in

time for him to see all the burnt sausages

on the floor.

Dad blamed my paper banger for guilty

making him drop the food,

while the cousins kept asking what was for

lunch now? hungry Uncle Kevin said,

 This is one **BIG** barbecue disaster!

Which was true but <u>not</u> very helpful (and it

really annoyed Dad).

I tried to make a suggestion but everyone was

distracted by ROOSTER

(Derek's dog).

Who suddenly JUMPED over the fence and snatched a sausage.

Dad suggested that he could put some more sausages on the barbecue as it was still hot? But Mum wasn't keen on that idea and neither was anyone else. ☹ Especially when the cousins pointed out how many ants were everywhere now.

Then Delia appeared and said,

Where's all the food?

Mum pointed to the ground, then to Rooster. Who was eating another sausage.

And THAT'S when I managed to

SAVE THE DAY ...

... by suggesting that maybe

we could get a takeaway instead?

TAKE AWAY

Yes, let's!   Yeah   At last   What-ever   Great idea   Lovely

It was the first time ALL day that anyone had really listened to me.

(Better late than never.)
The end.

Result!

There, now that's all done.

I'm about to do some more MONSTER doodling

when **M**r **F**ullerman
SPOTS what I'm up to.

He announces to the class that if we're
finished, we should

**"bring up your books to get them marked
straight away."**

I give him my book - and
hope for the best. ☺

Well done, Tom.
Very good work.

5 merits

Keep this up and you'll be
in NEXT MONTH'S newsletter
as well!

Mr Fullerman

I'd forgotten about my EXCELLENT*
DOODLE book cover being mentioned in the
NEWSLETTER - oh, and with the PHOTO
Mrs Mumble took too.

*See page 357 of Everything's Amazing (Sort Of)
for the whole story.

140

I'll have to get a few Extra copies and leave them lying around the house so Mum and Dad are reminded about my good work and will say nice stuff to me like,

Well done, Tom.

while proudly showing off the NEWSLETTER to THE FOSSILS. Who might even give me some extra pocket money for being such a GOOD hard-working grandson.

You're too kind, Granny.

Then Mum will put the NEWSLETTER on the fridge.

(And if she doesn't, I will.) Which will annoy Delia a lot.

I can't wait!

Mr Fullerman says unfortunately this

month's NEWSLETTER won't be ready to

take home for a few

reasons.

Photo-copier →

(a few reasons)

Luckily, I have

other things to think about as well as my

special mention in the NEWSLETTER. Like:

○ Who'll be picked to be a buddy? Me? Maybe? Maybe not

○ More genius ideas that annoy Delia

Guess who I am?   Very funny.

○ The NEW DOGZOMBIES video

Me, Derek and Norman want to make our very own **MUSIC** video for **DOGZOMBIES** (our BAND). We watch **DUDE 3** music videos all the time so thought it would be **AMAZING** and fun to make our own. We've been talking about it for ages.

Let's do a video

Derek's dad says he can help us. **W**hich is **OK** as long as he doesn't keep trying to **butt** in (like usual).

He's already been suggesting we watch a few more "classic music videos".

no

no

no

What do you mean you've never seen "Sledgehammer"?

I'm here

While I'm busy thinking of VIDEO ideas, Mr Fullerman **surprises** me by saying...

"You too, TOM, ARMS UP!"

Because he keeps making us do EXTRA SPORTS DAY practices when we're least

expecting it.

Like now.

It's making it VERY

difficult to finish

off my LARGE doodle. And Marcus keeps on telling Mr Fullerman when I'm drawing. (He's snitched quite a few times now.) Luckily for me, Marcus has been getting on Mr Fullerman's nerves too. He tells Marcus to get on with his own work.

Sir

Which I agree with. hummph

I've had to use ALL the excellent tricks I know to get this doodle finished.

Trick 1. Arranging books round me for cover. Always a good one. ⟶

Trick 2. Looking straight ahead at the same time as drawing. (Which takes a LOT of practice.)

Trick 3. Leaning over my work SO much Mr Fullerman can't see what I'm doing. Like this... Which seems to be working. Even Marcus can't see.

I'm upside down

WAFER
TREE

(As it's MATHS tomorrow, I'll probably have to start a new one to keep me going.)

BUDDIES

? Today we get to find

out about the buddies...

Oh, and there's maths too. ☹

(Doodle ideas ready if I get bored.)

It's not such a big deal if I don't get chosen.

I tell **AMY** she'll definitely get

picked. And she says, "I'm not so sure."

So I say, "How can you say that?"

And she says, "Who'd pick me?"

I tell **AMY**, "You wouldn't want to pick an

idiot, would you?"

"Thanks, Tom."

It's supposed to be a compliment, but from

the way **AMY** said "Thanks, Tom" maybe it

didn't sound like one.

Brmmm

Brmmm

Mr Fullerman is busy handing out letters about who's going to be a buddy and what they have to do.

Becoming a buddy

Being a buddy to some of the younger children is a very responsible role.
All buddies are expected to be: helpful, kind, good listeners with good advice.
Your teachers are there to help.
Remember to be the BEST buddy you can be!

Mr Keen

He tells the whole class, **"If you don't get chosen this time, you will have another chance next term."**

Then he hands a letter to ...

 and I say, "Told you!"

And then to ... ME!

Looks like I'm going to be a buddy to some kid in Class 2R?

Let me see who it is.

Joey Dawson.

That name rings a bell.

Marcus hasn't been chosen this time. He's peering over my shoulder to see who I've got.

He says, "Ha! Ha! That kid is trouble." And I say, "Well, I'm going to be a GOOD buddy and keep him out of trouble."

Then I remember who Joey Dawson is.

(I'm sure he's not like that ALL the time?)

Hooray, it's BREAK-TIME

I meet up with Derek and Norman, who have both been picked to be buddies. Derek says his buddy seems nice and Norman's buddy looks a bit like him (only smaller)

I can see Joey on the other side of the school grounds.

He's waving at me. I tell Derek and Norman that he's my buddy.

"Look, here he comes now."

We all watch Joey walk right through a game of football and not notice a thing. Which doesn't go down well with the other kids.

I want to make a good buddy impression, so I say, "Thanks for choosing me as your buddy, Joey!"

Joey smiles but doesn't say anything. I'm trying to remember what sort of stuff is in the letter, and what I'm supposed to be helping Joey with as his buddy.

I add...

"Got any worries about anything, Joey?"

He shakes his head no.

"Maybe school?"

Joey shakes his head again.

"Friends or teachers giving you a hard time?"

Joey shakes his head.

(This buddy business is going to be easy.)

T hen I ask him,

"Have you got any questions you want
to ask me?"

And Joey thinks for a bit ... and says,

"Yes, can I be in your band, please?"

Which takes ALL of us by surprise.

Huh!

I wasn't expecting that question.

So I tell Joey that we're not looking for new

band members right now.

"You can come to our next band practice

and watch us if you want?"

Joey says, "That would be **great.**"

Then he jumps up and down and punches the

air, saying, "YES! YES!" Which is funny!

...Until he accidentally

`BiFF'S`

YES

Mr Fullerman, who's walking past him on break duty. Mr Fullerman is NOT very happy because he's spilled his cup of tea as well.

He tells Joey, **"Joey, you must be more careful!"**

Then he adds, **"Tom, you're his buddy,** you should be looking out for him."

Like it was my fault! (It wasn't.)

Derek and Norman think it's a BAD idea to let Joey watch our band practice.

"He'll break something," Derek says.

"He's **worse** than **me**," Norman adds.

The band could definitely do with a practice and **another** gig.

The last time we played, it was for Granny Mavis and her Over 70S

and Make Group.

(Not sure it was a proper gig, though?) I promise Derek and Norman that if Joey turns up, I'll make sure he doesn't touch (or break) anything.

Don't move

(Don't know how ... but I'll try.)

(Granny's Over 70s Cake & Make)

NEWSLETTER

and other interesting facts

Mr Keen, our headmaster (or **RED** master, as I call him when he gets **CROSS**), told us in assembly that the NEWSLETTERS have all been posted to our parents now.

"Along with some other important information AND your mid-term REPORT CARDS!"

I'm hoping that the GOOD mention in the NEWSLETTER will make up for anything **dodgy** that might be **LURKING** in my → REPORT CARD. (Fingers crossed there's no mention of made-up LATE NOTES or that kind of thing.)

Mrs Nap goes on to tell everybody about the SCHOOL TALENT-SHOW AUDITIONS. She says we are hoping to see "LOTS OF YOU TALENTED CHILDREN ALL COMING ALONG FOR THE AUDITIONS!"

Mrs Nap explains, "This year's production is a talent show, so anyone can join in. AND there will only be one dress rehearsal once you've been chosen, unlike last year's play."

Which is good to know.

I managed to avoid last year's PLAY - unlike Solid.

(Solid as a tree. He was very good.)

Maybe **DOGZOMBIES** could be part of the show this year, especially with my NEW GUITAR, and because **DOGZOMBIES** can now play SIX whole songs all the way through. ♪ ♩ ♪

I can see it now...

Secret MESSAGES (Shhhhh)

Back in class,
Mr **F**ullerman has found
yet another way of making
us do EXTRA practice for
SPORTS DAY. We all have to Jump up
and touch the arrow before he lets us come
into class.

Then he explains to the class what
we'll be doing today.

Top jump
jump

First of all, you need to write the WHOLE
alphabet out, and underneath each letter,
make up your own symbols. Remember
when we looked at the Egyptian
hieroglyphics?

That's what I want you all to do.

I thought it sounded a bit dull. Zzzzzzzz yawn yawn... I was getting ready to start a new doodle ... when Mr Fullerman gave us some examples of a SECRET MESSAGE written in code.

We had to work out what the message said. It was BRILLIANT!

Crack the secret code below, then make up your OWN CODE for the alphabet.

A B C D E F G H I J K
L M N O P Q R S T U V
W X Y Z

Next, we have to invent our OWN CODE.
Which could be VERY useful, especially if I
don't want certain people to know what
I'm writing about...

Marcus is LOOKING
at what I'm doing and
SNIFFING right by my ear.
I tell him to stop doing both and he says, "I'm
busy concentrating on my own code" (he's not).
His pen has started to leak and it's
leaving ink on his hands, which
he keeps putting on his face.
I try and tell him what he's doing.
But he ignores me and says Whatever.
(I did try.)

Nosy

? Sniff

I spend the rest of the lesson making up my own

MONSTER ALIEN

code. Which I am VERY pleased with!

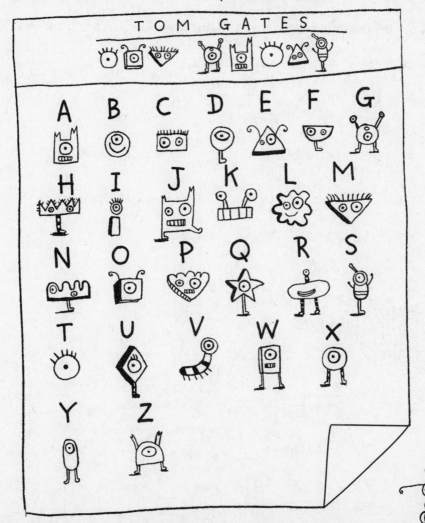

Once we've finished making up our own code, Mr Fullerman wants us to write a letter to the person sitting next to us. I write this one for Marcus, then pass him my ALPHABET so he can work out what it says.

It takes him a while.

Eventually he gets it.

Huh?_

Ha! Ha!

Joey

Buddy duties are proving to be trickier than I first thought. Every SINGLE break-time and lunchtime, Joey comes to say

Hello!

But that's ALL he says. (Joey doesn't talk much.) I tried to pass a few tips on about getting by in Oakfield School.

But it's hard to tell if he's interested or not.

Mr Fullerman is on break duty (again) and he's looking over in my direction. So I'm trying to show him that I'm being an excellent buddy.

168

I ask Joey if he'd like to have a game of
football with me and a few of my friends,
    "Just a little kick around."
And Joey nods YES.
    So I get a ball and ask Derek
and Solid to join in too. We're
kicking it to each other, nothing fancy.

Joey's actually pretty good at football. He's doing
OK. Mr Fullerman is still wandering around the
school grounds keeping an eye on everyone. And
(hopefully) noticing what a GOOD buddy I'm being.
I kick the football HIGH in the air and call out,
    "Joey ... on your head!" And Joey jumps up
and tries to HEAD the ball back to me...

Well, I think that's what he wanted to do.

The ball FLIES off his head in the opposite direction and lands right in ... Mr Fullerman's cup of tea.

Which spills EVERYWHERE (again).

Mr Fullerman says,

"For GOODNESS' sake, Tom, will you LOOK where you're kicking that ball!"

And I want to shout, "It WASN'T ME!"

But because I am a NICE buddy, I say..."Sorry, sir."

Marcus has been watching us and comes over.

Joey

He says, "I'm glad I don't have a buddy like yours."

And I say, "It was an accident, wasn't it, Joey?"

But Joey's already gone back into school to avoid **Mr Fullerman** and me (I think).

Marcus says, "I told you your buddy was trouble."

Thanks for that, Marcus.

On the way home from school, Derek gets out **TWO** caramel wafers.

"My buddy gave them to me for being nice." And I'm thinking I DESERVE **LOADS** of WAFERS for not snitching on Joey. (Who's been staying out of my way since the football incident.)

Derek gives me one of his wafers, which is nice of him. I try and make mine last all the way home by eating it in sections.

Like this

Break in half

Eat in sections

I'm just finishing the last tiny little bit when I open the front door, go into the kitchen and find THIS PINNED UP ON THE FRIDGE!

OAKFIELD SCHOOL
NEWSLETTER

ISSUE FOUR

WELL DONE
to **TOM GATES**
from Class 5F

For producing an excellent piece of homework - fantastic drawings in his sketchbook

NEW SCHOOL MASCOT

Yes, Oakfield School has a new visitor

CONGRATULATIONS!
to Adam and Zoe!

For a fabulous swim for Team Oakfield and bringing back a medal

My HEAD looks like a GIANT

PINEAPPLE.

(Shame.)

Mum says she is VERY pleased with me. But
we need to have a little CHAT about
a few other things when Dad finishes work.

(We do? That doesn't sound good.)

The only time Mum says things like that is if
I'm in trouble or if Delia has been blaming ME
for stuff I didn't do.

Who ate all the jam?

Empty

Tom did

Who used all the towels?

Tom did

Delia is upstairs LURKING around in the bathroom. I'm going to ask her what she's been saying about me NOW?

I wait for Delia to come out ...

... and when she does, I notice that her hair has turned a VERY odd colour. It looks a bit ... green?

It IS GREEN !

I follow ══════⟩ Delia into her room to
get a PROPER look.
But she shuts the door and tells me to

GET LOST!

I ask her through the closed door,
"What happened to your hair, Delia?"
And she tells me to

"Go AWAY, you're annoying."

So I say, "Did you know your hair's **GREEN**?"
Followed by,

"Why the **GREEN** hair?"

Delia says if I don't go away she'll tell Mum that I've been writing my own LATE NOTES How does she know that?

I go back to my room and while I'm thinking of excuses in case Mum and Dad ask me about my late note ... I have a

GENIus iIDEA

for a song.

Which goes like this...
(As I've written down the words, it seems a shame not to do some nice drawings to go with it?)

GREEN

AGH!

GREEN

Delia ... doesn't want to be SEEN

Because her hair has gone bright GREEN.

It looks the colour of a LEAF

Now Mum and Dad will give her GRIEF.

She tried to make her hair look FINE

But now it's gone a shade of LIME.

Delia ... she can be MEAN.
Delia ... her hair is GREEN.

I go back downstairs (still singing my new song) and Mum wants to know what I'm singing about.

Delia's GREEN hair.

Delia's clean hair?

And I say, No, green hair.

Then Dad comes in from his shed and *CONGRATULATES* me on being in the NEWSLETTER, then adds that we need to talk about a few other things too.

So I change the subject quickly and say, "Delia's got green hair."

Just then, **THE FOSSILS** (Granny Mavis and Granddad Bob) 'POP' in to say "hello". Like they do. And Granny says, "Who's got **GREEN** hair?"

And I say, "Delia."

Granddad laughs and says, "At least she's got hair, not like me!"

Then I add, Or Dad. Which is true, but Dad doesn't look too happy now.

Mum goes upstairs to see Delia, and Dad says he's off to get changed.

Granny Mavis mentions she's taken up knitting again. She says, "I could make Delia a **HAT** if she needs one?"

Which is a GREAT idea.

Maybe I should help Granny with a few hat ideas.

Like these...

(This one is my personal favourite.)

Dad suddenly appears wearing
THOSE shorts again.
He tells everyone "I'm going
for a brisk run," (like we wanted to know),

Then Mum comes back downstairs and says
that Delia's had a bit of a

HAIR-DYE DISASTER.

I say, "Really? I hadn't noticed." Mum says, "She's
probably been using some TERRIBLE cheap
hair dye. Not like the one I use."

I tell Mum that Granny Mavis has
offered to knit Delia a hat.

"To cover up her green HAIR."

Mum says,

Actually, Delia's quite upset about her hair and doesn't want to see anyone because she's feeling a bit...

And I say, Like a tree?

Mum gives me a **look** and says,

No, Tom, she's feeling a bit self-conscious and embarrassed.

Granny says "Poor Delia" then tells us they're off to the shops to pick up a few odds and ends.

(From the look of Granny's list, it's mostly "odd" things.)

Buy ingredients for
sausage and jam rolls

peach and pea soup

Raspberry & tomato PIE

Then Mum says BYE to **THE FOSSILS** who wish her **LUCK** sorting everything out.

Mum WAS being all nice and sympathetic about Delia's hair. Right up until she discovered

Poor Delia

it was **HER** hair dye Delia had been using. Now she's really **NOT** happy about that!

FAB HAIR DYE

FAB HAIR DYE

It's quite late when Dad gets back from his run. He looks **RED** in the face and is limping a bit. He says,

"I'm in agony, I think I've pulled a muscle."

Mum asks, "Is that part of your carefully planned fitness regime too?"

Then she says, "At least you have an excuse not to run in the

PARENTS' RACE on Tom's SPORTS DAY."

How did she know about my SPORTS DAY? I've been keeping it quiet. Especially after last year's race.

Dad

Mr Fingle →

(Last year's race) →

Puff
Puff

I say, "You don't HAVE to come, my class are always LAST anyway."

Dad says he'll be fine and he's looking forward to running and BEATING Derek's dad this time. (I'm not.)

Mum wants to know if I'm auditioning for the school talent show tomorrow as well?

How does she know about that?

"I read your NEWSLETTER and your mid-term→ REPORT CARD too."

Oh! Oh! My report card has arrived.

Dad says, Which reminds me, we want to talk to you about your report card, Tom.

(I'm getting worried now.)

Dad limps over to get it. I can't remember anything **BAD** that I've done (apart from the LATE NOTE and a few other notes too).

Mum and Dad are both looking at me with very serious faces. They say, "Tom, we are very surprised that..."

You are an idiot.

"You're doing **SO WELL!** It's amazing. Well done! Keep it **UP!**"

WOW! That's a first for me. My report card usually says things like:

Tom does too much chatting/doodling. Tom doesn't do enough homework/ maths.

But now on a scale of Idiot to Genius I'm about here.

Mum thinks I should put my guitar to good use and enter **DOGZOMBIES** in the talent show. "You're doing so well at everything!"

Good point. Maybe we could do it?

I give **N**orman a ring first and then **D**erek to see if they agree.

Let's!

Yeah

They do.

While I'm on the phone to Derek, I remind him about last year's parents' race and how embarrassing it was watching our dads run.

Then I have a **Terrible** thought. "Cycling shorts ... my dad could turn up wearing those cycling shorts!"

Derek says,

"Shame."

While we're chatting on the phone, I can hear Rooster in Derek's garden running around **barking** like MAD. Derek says Rooster's been chewing all his socks, which is driving him **BONKERS.** And I suddenly think of an excellent way to avoid a possible SPORTS DAY cycling shorts shame after all.

(Genius idea.)

SPORTS DAY!

Now Dad's cycling shorts have miraculously disappeared, I'm fine with him and Mum both coming to my SPORTS DAY.

I'd better remember to bring ALL my own sports kit (for good reason). On the way to school, Derek tells me that his dad has actually been

Wear this

practicing for the parents' race.

He has? Wow, that's embarrassing.

Before we go to the sports ground, Mr Fullerman gives the whole class what he calls a **motivational talk.**

 His eyes look even bigger than usual because he is all enthusiastic.

GO FOR IT, CLASS 5F! TRY YOUR BEST AND HAVE FUN.

I say to **AMY**,

"**W**hat he really means is ... don't be rubbish and come last again."

Which is true.

The sports grounds are divided up into sections for all the different "sports" we'll be doing. Mrs Worthington RINGS a big BELL to start off each "sport" or race. Every class gets points for:

Goals scored

Beanbags caught

Balls bounced

Long jumps taken

Hulas hooped

When all the classes have done every "sport", ☆ the points are added up and the WINNERS are announced – after the parents' race, of course.

Mr Sprocket's class are wearing vests with SLOGANS on so they look like a proper team.

We just look like ... Class 5F.
Mrs Worthington rings the bell)) to begin the first session.

Solid gets us off to a good start with a spectacular hula hoop. Mark Clump and Amber Tulley Green don't do badly either. It's not my favourite "sport", but I manage to add a few points as well.

Go

Solid

Go Solid

Beanbag catching is a **disaster.** We're missing them all over the place. Beanbags are flying everywhere! Thankfully, Leroy Lewis and Ross White do a really good job catching theirs for Class 5F.

Marcus is complaining about feeling all "itchy" when he KEEPS on missing the basketball challenge.

197

And he blames me for -*shoving* him, which I did (accidentally).

Mr Fullerman seems to be smiling, which is better than last year. Oh well

AMY and Indrani are telling Julia that she's doing really well and not to be nervous about the long jump, which is our last sport.

It's not helping that Mr Sprocket is leading his class in a LOUD...

Give me a **W**

Give me an **I**

Give me an **N**

Give me another **N**

Give me an **E**

Give me an **R**

Give me an **S**

What have you got?

There's a slight pause as none of the class can work out what they've just spelled. In the end it's Mr Fullerman who says...

"It spells WINNERS, but don't count on it"

to Mr Sprocket's class.

Mr Fullerman's SPORTS DAY

training starts paying off, as we're doing very

well in the beanbag relay race.

Mr Keen is wandering around saying

encouraging things like:

"Perfect pass, Pansy" and

"Really fast run, Robert."

There are lots of families, friends and parents on one side of the grounds behind a barrier who are *cheering* too.

I can't see 👁 👁 anyone from my family ... yet. Mrs Worthington rings the bell for everyone to stop for:

Drinks, oranges and BISCUITS.

Which is VERY popular. During the break, Mr Fullerman tells us that everyone is doing BRILLIANTLY and we're definitely NOT going to come last this year.

Yes! Yes!

(I think he's more pleased than we are.)

(201)

Norman has somehow managed to eat **WAY** too many biscuits. And as the sugar starts to **kick** in, he's rolling around on the ground with his legs in the <u>air</u> saying...

Look, I'm a dying fly!

"Yes, you are, Norman."

(Oh dear.)

The last sport for Class 5F is the **long** jump. I still can't see any of my family in the crowd at **all**. Until **AMY** says,

You're popular.

I glance over to where Amy's looking.

Now I can see ...

... AND HEAR them.

(Shame.)

I manage to get **THE FOSSILS** not to wave the

WE LOVE YOU, TOM banner.

Luckily, I'm not the only one with an

embarrassing family. Julia Morton's parents are

wearing T-shirts ...

 with her FACE on

them.

Which hasn't helped her feel

any less **NERVOUS**. Oh NO!

Mrs Worthington rings the

bell and says, "It's time

for the last sport.

GOOD luck!"

Which is LONG JUMP in our case.

I take my turn ... run as

fast as I can and ...

...throw myself into the sand pit. Yes

It's not a bad j u m p either.

Good enough for THE FOSSILS to take out

the WE LOVE YOU, TOM banner again.

Yeah

Most of the class have jumped and there's just TWO kids to go.
Mr Fullerman (who's been having a sneaky peek ⊂⊃ ⊂⊃ at the scores) says,

Only a few points between Mr Sprocket's class and us now.

Which is good news.

 The last TWO jumps need to be as LONG as POSSIBLE!

Julia Morton and Marcus say
But I'm not sure they're
feeling confident.

OK

Marcus goes first. The class start clapping to help him jump further. When he starts running, they all say...

"Whhhhhooooooooooooooo!"

until he lands.

Then it's an, "Ooooooooh?" as his long jump is ... only a tiny bit better than last time.

Itchy →

Marcus says he got distracted in mid-air by his ITCHY T-shirt. (If you say so, Marcus.)

Then Julia goes to jump. She looks very NERVOUS.

The class go...

Whhhhhoooo

Because Julia's jump is AMAZING!
We're all cheering and clapping. But we won't
know who's won the SPORTS DAY trophy
until after the parents' races.
(I'd forgotten about that)

Just like last year, some dads are taking the race a LOT more seriously than others. My dad is trying to pretend the race is

Just a bit of *FUN*.

But from the Determined LOOK on his face and the fancy running shoes he's wearing, I can tell he wants to WIN.

Mrs Worthington sets them off with a whistle ≡3 this time.

Fancy trainers

Dad manages to HUFF and PUFF himself into ...

THIRD PLACE!

(Embarrassing headband)

PUFF

YES!

Ahead of Derek's dad (Mr Fingle), which he is VERY pleased about.

I say to Derek, "Phew, over for another year!" And Derek says, "I can't believe my dad wore that headband."

(I'm guessing Rooster might have something else to play with later.)

Mum says she can't run in the "mums' race" because she's worn the wrong shoes (accidentally on purpose, I think).

whoops!

Now the **FOSSILS** want to know why there isn't a grandparents' race too? (I'm sort of glad there isn't, to be honest.)

M_r K_{een} comes over and says they have added up ALL the points and are ready to announce the

"winner of this year's
SPORTS DAY **Trophy, who is ...**

Class 5N!"

It's Mrs Nap's class ... and we're SECOND. In front of Mr Sprocket's class. But from the way Mr Fullerman is leaping around and

cheering

you'd think it was us who had won.

I've never seen him so happy.

The VERY **best** thing about coming **second** at SPORTS DAY is that Mr Fullerman is in an EXCELLENT ⟨mood⟩ 😊 for the rest of the week.

He has made a special SPORTS DAY DISPLAY, which is ...

SECOND 5F THIRD 5S

Sports Day was won this year by 5N

Everyone who took part had a fantastic time. Especially 5F and Mr Fullerman.

SECOND WERE CLASS 5F

... right outside Mr Sprocket's classroom.

**Sports Day
Winners 5N**

The morning of the auditions for the school Talent Show

I'm a bit achy

after SPORTS DAY. (All that

jumping into sandpits and catching beanbags.)

On the way to school Derek and I discuss

the audition and what song we should play.

Derek says it has to be "Smoke on the Water".

And I say, Why's that?

And Derek says, "Because the old folks loved

that song and Mrs Nap and Mr Sprocket are

quite old so they'll like it too."

Good point. ➡️

"Smoke on the Water"
Old folks enjoying the song

I've brought my new guitar to school. And I'm a bit nervous that something might happen to it. I get even more worried when the first person we see is ...

Joey.

He's not been around much since the football incident. But because I am a GOOD buddy, I say, Hi, Joey and tell him we're auditioning for the school talent show. He says, I'll see you there.

He will?

Straight away I'm thinking, I'll have to keep an EXTRA eye on my guitar. I don't want anything happening to it with Joey around.

In class, I ask **Mr Fullerman** if he could keep his beady eyes ⊙ ⊙ on my guitar until it's time for the auditions. I don't ask him like THAT.

Obviously.

Please, Mr Fullerman, could you keep my guitar in a safe place?

AMY, Indrani and Florence are all singing ♪♪♩ for their audition. I ask Marcus what he's doing and he says,

"A magic act that I've been practicing a LOT. So it's really good."

And I say, Can you do any magic now?

And he says no because he needs his special box of magic tricks. Which sounds interesting.

I tell Marcus that my granddad taught me how to do a really good

and I can show

him if he wants?

Marcus says,

"Go on, then ... impress me."

MY GRANDDAD'S MAGIC TRICK

Empty

Granddad's trick goes like this...

1. Take a tissue and **scrunch** it up in your hand, then say

> I can make it *disappear*.

2. Then stand up and hold the tissue in your hand. Move your hand up and down while counting to four like this.

One... Two... Three...

Four...

3. Then on the fourth or fifth time, LET GO of the tissue by throwing it behind the person's head so they don't see it.

Now open your hand really slowly to show that the tissue has DISAPPEARED.

It does take a bit of practice.

Gone

But it worked really well on Marcus.

School
Talent Show
AUDITIONS

Joey comes to our classroom to collect us for our audition because he is helping Mr Sprocket.

I hold on to my guitar tightly and say, "Hi, Joey." He nods hello.

Ready?

We're walking to the hall when Norman says, "**DUDE 3** are definitely coming to play here because the whole school are talking about it."

And I say, "I hope it's **TRUE**, Norman. It would be **SO** good."

(Rumours often start in school that aren't true.)

Rumour in school

What really happened

Derek is already waiting for us along with Marcus (who's auditioning next).

Marcus is wearing ... a **CAPE**.

He's swishing it around and trying to be all dramatic.

Mr Sprocket calls out,

DOGZOMBIES NEXT, PLEASE.

But before we can start, Mr Sprocket asks for help

carrying some chairs and checking the drum kit is at the right height first, please.

We have no choice.

Just prop your guitar over there for a second, Tom.

I'm NOT going to do THAT! So Joey offers to hold it. And I have to stop myself from saying,

NO WAY!

Then MARCUS says, I'll look after it.

Which is only a tiny bit better than Joey, but I don't have much of a choice. So while we go with Mr Sprocket to pick up the chairs and a few music stands, Marcus is left holding my guitar. Like this... ➡

I can see ⊙⊙ him FIDDLING with the strings! I tell him, "Don't touch the strings." But he ignores me. Now he's TWIDDLING with the end of [my] guitar and doing ROCK STAR poses while pretending to play it. I can't take my guitar back FAST enough!

(227)

Marcus says, "Don't snatch."
Guitar in hand – we get ready for our audition.

Hello – we're **DOGZOMBIES**.

But when I start to play "SMOKE ON THE WATER", it doesn't sound like "Smoke on the Water". It sounds **TERRIBLE**.

My guitar has gone out of tune because Marcus was fiddling **SO MUCH** with the strings. I have to keep going.

But it's a rotten audition. I can tell from the faces Mr Sprocket and Mrs Nap are pulling. They look like they're in pain.

When we've finished, Mr Sprocket says,

> Well done. Just a few tuning issues to be sorted out ... but not bad, boys.

Which is better than I thought. Derek tells me not to worry. Norman says,

> It wasn't so bad.

Marcus says, "What happened? You lot were RUBBISH! More like DOG'S DINNER than DOGZOMBIES."

Which is irritating ... but true. Derek says, "Thanks, Marcus. Let's see how YOU do, then?" Marcus SWISHES his cape and goes off to perform.

(229)

He announces himself as "MAGIC MARCUS".

Which sounds like MAGIC MARKERS and makes us all LAUGH. Ha! Ha! Ha!

Marcus is doing tricks with cards and all kinds of different things and is surprisingly good, which is a bit annoying.

Now Joey has brought along AMY, Florence and Indrani for their audition.

"How did you do?" Amy asks me.

I was about to say, "Not bad ... or OK, but might have done better" when Joey decides to **BUTT** in and tells **AMY**,

They were **TeRRIBLe,** all out of tune. ♪♪♪

Thanks, Joey! He's normally quiet. Some buddy he turned out to be. It wasn't my fault the guitar went out of tune. ♪♪♪

I tell Derek and Norman that

 "Marcus will probably go around telling EVERYONE how BAD DOGZOMBIES were."

And Derek says, Do you think so?

Yes, that's EXACTLY what Marcus does.

Hopeless, they were

Shame

DOGZOMBIES were RUBBISH

Oh dear

It was painful to listen to

Now ALL the school are talking about DUDE 3 playing at the school talent show. AND the RUBBISH audition DOGZOMBIES did.

Which was THE WORST audition EVER in the WHOLE HISTORY of the school.

(That last bit's not true ... but that's what it FEELS like everyone is saying.)

It's [not] very long before the list of successful AUDITIONS gets pinned up on the school notice board. Somehow ... DOGZOMBIES has made it.

Oakfield School Talent Show Audition Results

If your name is below, you're in the SHOW!
We'll have ONE dress rehearsal before the show.

Well done, EVERYONE

Brad Galloway	Indrani Hindle
Julia Morton	Florence Mitchell
Minnie Verner	Paul Rogers
June Rawlings	Jenny Chan
Tom Gates	Christina Brown
Norman Watson	Roger Wood
Derek Fingle	Emily Border
Marcus Meldrew	Chad Dury
Amy Porter	Paul Jolly

SPECIAL GUEST APPEARANCE TO BE ANNOUNCED

In fact, looking at the list, I think **everyone** who auditioned made it.

Right at the bottom it says

SPECIAL GUEST APPEARANCE

to be announced.

Which looks interesting?

Could the RUMOURS be true after all?

Family
Outing to the
CINEMA

$\stackrel{\cdots}{O}$n the way home we BUMP$\stackrel{\cdots}{\cdots}$ into Joey going the other way.

(When I say we bumped into him ... I mean we BUMPED into him.)

I ask him if he's OK?

He nods. Then he says,

When can I come to your band practice?

I'd forgotten about that.

And I'm looking at Derek, who seems a bit alarmed.

I tell Joey that we're SUPPOSED to be filming our BAND [VIDEO] soon.

It might not be a good time to come and watch us. Sorry. ☹

Joey says,

 I could come and help you and bring WAFERS.

And Derek shrugs his shoulders like it's OK with him. So I say, "OK, Joey, it'll be at Derek's house. I'll let you know when."

Joey says, "Yeah, thanks." Then he runs off and bumps into someone else coming around the corner.

AGH! Whoops

W hen I get home M um reminds me

that we're supposed to be having some

 QUALITY family time together tonight.

And I say, We are?

"Yes, we're going to the cinema. We have to go somewhere dark or D elia won't come with us while her hair's still a bit :GREEN."

"W hat are we seeing?"

M um says it's a great film that's had lots of good reviews.

 "It's called The tter."

Aand I say, What's it about?

Because I've never heard of the film?

Then Delia butts in and she says,

It's about an OTTER, stupid.

So I say, "Not necessarily, it could be a film about SPIES and

'THE OTTER' is a code name for a secret agent."

And Delia says,

"OR it could be about an OTTER and that's why there's a MASSIVE

picture on the film poster of AN OTTER."

Mum says,

"All right, Delia,

that's enough."

Then I suggest that if Delia doesn't
want to be seen with her GREEN
hair, she could always ask Granny Mavis to
knit one of these hats for her?

Like this
or this.

Then Dad comes
in and says,

Has anyone seen
my cycling shorts?
I can't find them
any where.

This seems like a good time to disappear to
my room and wait until we're all ready to go.

Which takes AGES.

We're so late we nearly miss the start of the film. As we're buying the tickets, Mum is getting STRESSED because she likes to sit near the ⟶ FRONT of the cinema and she's worried it will all be FULL. And she HATES it when people eat too LOUDLY. Mum thinks there should be RULES for what you can eat in the cinema.

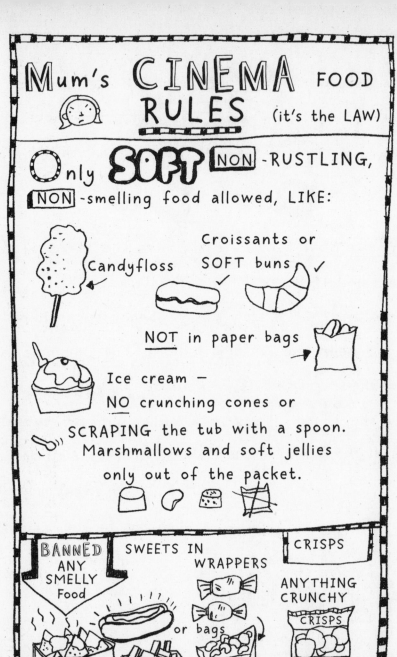

I've brought a few fruit chews that I unwrap
BEFORE the film starts. Otherwise Mum will
keep STARING and nudging
me until I stop.

We all manage to get seats near the
front before the film starts. Delia has got
her hood up and looks even more grumpy than
usual. I tell Dad that I don't want to

Grump
→

sit next to her if she's taking
off her sunglasses again.

So Dad sits between us.

We're all settled
and the lights are just going down. Mum's
happy with her seat. There's no one eating too
LOUDLY near us. Everything is great.
When this happens to me...

(243)

I can't see a thing now!

That's just great. I keep moving from side
to side but I still can't see the film.
Mum tells me to (stop fidgeting,
Tom.

SWAPPED

I say, "I can't see."
So Mum swaps seats with
me. And for about a
minute I can see the
whole screen.

Then the TALLEST man in
the world with the
← BIGGEST head does
this ... and that's when I
realize who's sitting in front
of me.

It's Solid and HIS DAD.

I tap him on the back and say, "Hi!" And Mum says, "Shhhhhh."

I decide to go and sit next to him because I can't see anything behind him or his dad.

The film is REALLY Funny. Even Delia is laughing (but I'm not going to look at her without her glasses again).

Mum keeps tapping me on the head every time Solid and I chat. Even a tiny bit.

Solid says, "Are your whole family here?"

And I whisper,

"Yes, we're having quality family time watching a film. So we don't have to talk to each other."

Then Mum Taps me on the head again and tells me to...

Shhhhhhhhh...

Groan

When the film is finished, Dad says he's going to the toilet and he'll meet us outside. We all get up to leave and Solid and I are **chatting** about the film, our SPORTS DAY and the school auditions, STUFF like that.

It's only when he says BYE and walks off with his dad that I realize how similar they both are.

Solid

His dad

Mum wants to know what's taking Dad so long and she goes off to find him, leaving me outside with Delia (who's getting grumpier).

Then suddenly Delia *Huh!* notices that **E**d, her old boyfriend, is coming out of the cinema with some of his friends. She tells me, "Don't move or **ELSE**." And ducks behind me.

I decide to have some fun and start moving from side to side so Delia has to follow me. I can hear Delia whispering behind me, "Don't you DARE" as Ed looks up and sees me. I wave and say, "Hi, Ed, fancy seeing you here."

Ed comes over and says, "Hi, Tom." And I say, "Good film, wasn't it?" and he says, "Great ... are you still in your band?"

And I say, "Yes, thanks."

Delia's still crouched down with her hood covering her GREEN hair and she's trying to sneak away without Ed noticing. Which might have worked if I hadn't moved out of the way at exactly the same time as a

BIG $gust$ of wind $SWEEPS$ Delia's hood right off her head. Delia's GREEN hair stands out a LOT.

(250)

Everyone is looking at her – including Ed.
Mum and **D**ad come back just in time to
stop Delia from taking her **REVENGE**
on me. She says, "You wait."

Which doesn't sound good.

So I suggest Delia lightens up
and has some **FUN.** "Like me!"
Mum says it's nice that we're
both enjoying ourselves.
(Well, I am... Delia looks a bit grumpy and
GREEN still.)

With all the stuff that's been going on in school, it's easy to forget about my...

Homework?

Because **M**r **F**ullerman is STILL in a super good mood from SPORTS DAY, he says I can bring it in tomorrow. Which is good news for me.

I've been spending **LOADS** of my time at home (and in class) PLANNING and thinking of ideas for the DOGZOMBIES VIDEO.

Planning for the video

WILD Thing Video

There are SO many things we could do. Like:

o Make **WILD THING** masks.

WILD THING

o Make WILD THING posters to put in the background.

o Film in the garden, which looks a bit jungley in parts.

I've got LOADS of IDEAS going on in my head. And writing a WHOLE A4 page about "MY SPORTS DAY" just isn't one of them.

"Tomorrow" has come round a bit **too** quickly – I've only managed to write a bit of my homework while on the way to school this morning.

I have to finish it off under my desk ... and on my lap ... so **Mr Fullerman** can't see what I'm doing.

Under the circumstances I think I've done OK?

My Sports Day
By TOM GATES

I REALLY LIKED SPORTS DAY THIS YEAR BECAUSE WE NEARLY WON! YEAH! AND MR FULLERMAN HAS BEEN IN A GOOD MOOD.

WE HAD NICE ORANGE BISCUITS, WHICH WAS A TREAT. YEAH!

Tom ....

Y o u   s e e   e   m
   t   o   b   e
s p a c i n g
o   u   t   your words a lot?

This does not fool me into thinking
you have done a whole A4 page!

Don't try this again.

Mr Fullerman

Phew ... could have been worse.

No detention or mention of "EXTRA WORK".

256

DOGZOMBIES VIDEO

After an **EXHAUSTING** week at school, me, Norman and Derek are very busy making some important decisions about the **DOGZOMBIES** video that we're filming today.

1. Hats or no hats?

2. Sunglasses or no sunglasses?

3. Outside or inside?

4. Masks or no masks?

5. Wafers now or later? Cool!

Wafers later is the only decision we've made so far. Mostly because we don't want Norman to peak too soon.

I say, "What do you think would do if they were making this video?" Derek says he doesn't think they'd wear masks.

It's a good point. We stick to the **DOGZOMBIES** T-shirts instead and film inside Derek's garage, as it looks like it might rain. Mr Fingle has offered to help out and has set up the camera on his fancy Tripod. Which is great. But it does mean we can't move around much or we won't be in shot.

Derek's dad starts talking about **classic music videos of our time.**

AGAIN.

So Derek has to remind him that we're just doing this for fun. We're saved when Mr Fingle's phone rings - which keeps him busy for a bit. Derek says, "Shall we just press record on the camera and have a go then?"

It's a good plan. But we can't work out who's going to do it, because it's tricky pressing record, then running back into shot. We're just about to start filming when this time MRS Fingle comes in! She says, "You have a visitor to see **DOGZOMBIES**!" We do?

(259)

Hello It's Joey.

Who I invited round to watch us

do a band practice ... and then

forgot all about.

Come round tomorrow

Ok

Joey says his mum will

be picking him up in two hours.

And Derek says,

"TWO HOURS!"

like it's a really really long time. Then Joey

shows us a very small cool camera that his

mum has lent him to use today. "I can do

some filming too if you want?"

Which is an excellent idea.

(Joey's turning out to be really helpful after all.)

Though Joey does *knock* the tripod over
twice.

whoops

Mr Fingle comes back and starts making a
few filming suggestions.
Some are better than others...

Stand on one leg
... then PLAY!

Really?

But it does make **TWO** HOURS
WHIZZ by.

J oey's mum turns up just as we're really

Joey's
mum →

getting into filming. She says,

"This looks good! I'll help you put the

video together if you want."

Norman says, "**SWEET**."

(He means that's good.)

Then Joey says, "That reminds me - I brought

you these."

He throws me a whole pack of

caramel WAFERs!

YEAH! Then knocks over the camera for the THIRD time.

Camera!

Mr Fingle's checking his camera's still working (it is). I'm thinking Joey has turned out to be an excellent buddy after all.

Bye!

TALENT SHOW → rehearsal

Mr Fullerman reminds us that there's a

"RUN-THROUGH today for the school talent show before the REAL show, which is ... tonight."

I whisper to **AMY,** Tonight! Is he sure?

And **Mr Fullerman** says, **"Yes, Tom, tonight."**

How could I have forgotten when the school production was?

TALENT SHOW is THIS THURSDAY. DON'T FORGET!

SCHOOL NOTICE BOARD

TALENT

TALENT SHOW TONIGHT Special Guests

The GOOD news is DOGZOMBIES rehearsal time is at 11:15. It looks like I'll be missing ... MATHS. ☺ Result! (Making the DOGZOMBIES video was a bit of extra practice for us too, which is good.)

Marcus has his run-through before us at eleven o'clock. He's sitting next to me complaining (as usual). He thinks he should be on last. And I say, "How do you work that one out, Marcus?" and he says, "Because my act is the best one." And I say, "It might not be?"

And he says, "No one else is doing magic tricks like me."

And I say, "What about the **SPECIAL** **GUESTS**?

There's a **RUMOUR** that **DUDE 3** are coming to our school. They're better than you."

And he says, "Don't be **STUPID** ... **DUDE 3** won't come to our school. That's not going to happen, is it?"

Then he starts **SCRATCHING** his back, which makes ME feel itchy too. I stop scratching when I notice **AMY**, Indrani and Florence are looking at me.

They are getting ready to sing after **DOGZOMBIES**, followed by Mark Clump.

Who apparently is bringing in one of his **pets** that he's trained to do tricks.

(Maybe his snake? Which would be impressive.)

Brad is doing street dancing (not behind **Mr Fullerman's** back this time either).

I *wish* I knew who the **SPECIAL GUESTS** were!

If it's NOT **DUDE 3** ... who can it be? Mr Sprocket and Mrs Nap are not saying a word at the run-through.

They tell me...

"You'll have to wait and see like

everyone else, Tom."

Which is irritating. Because I wanted

to go home and tell Delia that

DUDE 3 were coming to our concert tonight.

She's not going out much because

of her (slightly) GREEN hair.

But it would still annoy her to miss them.

And I would remind her how she'd missed

them ... a lot.

Ha!

Oh well ... it can't be DUDE 3, can it?

Norman MUST have got

that wrong.

At lunchtime Joey comes to find me and he

says he's got a finished film of us playing

"WILD THING".

"I'll ask my mum to send it to you,

it's really good." ☺

(I am a GENIUS for getting Joey as a

buddy – OK, I know he picked me, but it's still

worked out well.)

High five

B̲ecause of the school production, everybody is allowed to go home an hour earlier to get ready.

W̲hich doesn't take me and Derek long to do.

BEFORE

AFTER

D̲erek is round at my house and we're looking at some copies of **ROCK WEEKLY** when I suggest that if we're going to look more like a **ROCK** band, I should wear some "shades

270

or SPIKE up my hair ... like this?"

And he says, "Do you think so?"
It might be a good idea.

I go into the bathroom and
help myself to some hair gel
that's been there for a while.
I think Uncle Kevin bought
it as a present for Dad ... as
a joke.
I still have a selection
of Delia's
sunglasses that we can
"borrow" for tonight, which both Derek and I
think we look pretty good in.

Derek stays at mine for some dinner and while we're eating, Dad comes in holding a plastic bag. He says, "I've got myself some new shorts for running."

Which he's pleased about.

I whisper to Derek, "Let's hope Rooster's still hungry."
Which makes him laugh.

TALENT → SHOW TONIGHT

(PLUS SPECIAL GUESTS!)

Chat
Chat

All the kids that are performing tonight are getting ready in the classrooms near the hall. There's a **lot** of excited chatting going on before the show starts. Me, Derek and Norman are all wearing our **DOGZOMBIES** T-shirts.

I show Norman the hair gel and say, "I think I should spike up my hair to look cooler and more like a

ROCK STAR"

And **AMY**, who's with Florence, hears me and says, "You should do it, Tom! That would look really good!" Norman just says,

YEAH!

because he's already getting a bit twitchy (like he does).

So I get a big handful of hair gel and put it in my hair, where it stays in a big

Derek says, "I think you need to rub it
in a bit."

Which I do. "What now?"

 AMY and Florence are looking
at my hair. Florence says,
"Maybe you should spike it up using a brush?"
But I don't have one. **AMY** says I can
borrow her brush, which is nice
of her. Now I've got half a
 of hair gel in my hair, I must
look a bit silly.

Derek suggests I
go and find a mirror so you can see
what you're doing.

(Good thinking.) I head to the toilet and try
to SPIKE up my hair using **AMY**'s funny
little round brush.

I've never used one of these before.

I twiddle it round the front of my hair, then try and drag it up^{wards} into a SPIKE.

But it's STUCK. So I twist it round a bit more. Which doesn't work at all. This is NOT good. I'm trying not to PANIC. But the more I twist the brush, the more tangled up it gets.

This is turning out to be a DISASTER!

I'm taking so long

that Derek comes

to find me.

He says, "We need

to get ready now, Tom." And I say, "There's

a tiny bit of a problem."

And Derek says, "I know, Mr Sprocket

wants us to go on early because of Marcus."

I don't think Derek has realized that

the brush I'm holding in my hand is actually

STUCK. I keep trying to get the brush

out while asking,

 "What's the problem with

Marcus?"

Derek says, "Mr Sprocket wants us to perform **FIRST** because Marcus has got…"

 I say,

"Nervous? … Cold feet? …

More annoying than ever?"

Derek says,

"No, not quite. He's cancelled because he's got…"

"A bit of a "**RASH**" ."

(Marcus scratching.)

Derek tells me his mum called and said it's not serious, but Marcus says he can't do his tricks because he's all ITCHY.

itchy →

(Marcus on SPORTS DAY)

"

That explains a lot.

Finally, Derek notices the brush sticking out of the top of my hair.

"What's wrong with your hair, Tom?"

"The brush is stuck,"

I say.

Derek has a go at trying to pull the brush out. I say "AGHHHH!" so he stops.

"How did you do THAT?"

"I twisted the brush and now it's stuck ... the hair gel made it worse."

I need to get help ... FAST!

But no one knows what to do.

Not even Mr Sprocket or Mrs Nap can get the brush out of my hair.

Mrs Mumble comes over. She says, "Joey got a comb stuck JUST like that."

"How did you get the comb out, Mrs Mumble?"

Mrs Mumble makes a scissor-cutting movement with her fingers.

"His mum had to cut the comb out. It was the only way, I'm afraid."

That's just great, then. GROAN...

Mr Sprocket says that we can go on later if I need the time to sort out the brush.

I say, "YES - we need LOADS more time." (Like a WEEK.)

Mr Sprocket says I will have to get my mum or dad to help now. Derek says he could go and look for my mum in the audience if I want.

"They should be here by now?"

Reluctantly, I say OK.

(283)

Mum takes one look at me and the brush and
says, "How did you manage to do **that**, Tom?"
I say, "It's a mystery, I just brushed my hair."
(I don't mention the half 🔲ton of hair gel.)
AMY is feeling a bit guilty because
it was her idea to use the brush.
She says, "I don't need it
back if you have to **BREAK**
it."

I really hope Mum's not
going to do THAT!

Hi ya!

But the only pair of scissors that anyone can find to cut my hair with are a bit **BLUNT**, with round tips that are meant for paper.

 Mum says, "I CAN'T use those, Tom."

So I have to either:

o   Ignore the brush (bit tricky).

o   Wear a BIG hat.

o   Wear a mask.

I don't want to go on stage with this brush **BOUNCING** around on my head.

The TALENT show has already started and seems to be going OK without Marcus.

Mr Keen made an announcement that there might be a few changes to the running order of the show.

We're now going to play LAST, so I'm hoping my hairbrush problem will be ALL sorted by then.

Ta da!

But it's not looking good.

Norman and Derek are shaking their heads and staring at me.

"This isn't working, is it, Tom?" Derek says.

He's right.

I don't want to go and play "WILD THING" in front of the school with a BRUSH sticking out of my hair.

I tell Mr Sprocket and Mrs Nap that I'm REALLY sorry, but I won't be able to play now.

"Never mind, Tom, We'll get the SPECIAL GUESTS to go on earlier," Mrs Nap says.

I'm thinking this could actually turn out to be really GREAT, because Mrs Nap knows I'm a DUDE 3 fan. I ask her, "Are DUDE 3 coming to play, then?" and she says, "That would be telling!"

Which probably means NO.

Mum goes back to her seat to watch the rest of the show (even though I'm not playing any more). She says she'll deal with the brush when I get home. (Shame.)

At least I get to watch the other talent-show performances that I didn't see before.

Like Mark Clump and his talking budgie.

Florence, **AMY** and Indrani singing.

(They're really good!)

Brad Galloway's EXCELLENT dancing.

Some little kids each doing

a line from a poem

(which takes a bit of time).

A few more singers.

And **A**ctors.

And a **V**entriloquist.

(My favourite so far.)

When the last performance is over, Mr Keen

comes on and all the lights go down.

He says it's been a wonderful show with SO many talented children from Oakfield School.

Clap

"I'm sure you're all wondering who the **SPECIAL GUESTS** are tonight?"

Clap

Clap

Clap **YESSSSSSSS!**

"Well, we are VERY privileged to welcome a WORLD-FAMOUS band to our school for a one-off performance – for the very **first** and possibly the **LAST** time."

And I'm looking at Derek and Norman, who've come to see who it is as well.

Norman says, Told you **DUDE3** were coming.

But I can't see them anywhere. Then Mr Keen says,

"We need to give a BIG OAKFIELD SCHOOL WELCOME to the one and only..."

(Drum rolIIIIIIIIIIIIIIIIIIII ... keep rolIIIIinggggggggggg...)

"YOU3!"

And for a split second I think Mr Keen has said and I'm jumping up and down and cheering when I see ...

Leather trousers

Mr Fullerman, Mr Sprocket and Mrs Worthingtash, dressed like they're going to ride motorbikes.

Mrs Worthington has on a FALSE MOUSTACHE (well, I <u>hope</u> it's false).

Me, Norman and Derek look SHOCKED.

Like this...

They start singing...

Get your lesson ready
Head out to the classroom
Get the children running
Practicing for SPORTS DAY

We're a NEW teachers' band
Who are born to be MILD
We can keep our cool
In Oakfield School

BORN TO BE MILD.

BORN TO BE MILD.

It's a funny song ... some of the adults are LAUGHING extra hard!
   Mr Sprocket and Mr Fullerman are stomping around pretending to be **ROCK** stars. But it's MRS WORTHINGTON who's going CRAZY!

I say to Derek, "This is the MADDEST thing ever!"
It might not be DUDE3, but **You3** are so hilarious I almost forget about the brush stuck in my hair.
Then the WHOLE school Clap and Cheer when they finish playing.
CLAP! Hooray CLAP! Hooray

I think the kids in our school will be talking about this teachers' performance
FOR EVER!

Thank you and goodnight

Now the show's over I say bye to everyone and go and meet up with Mum and Dad, who both think the teachers' band was "VERY good!" Dad says, "Makes me want to be in a band!"

Mum gives him a look 👁👁 and says, "I don't think so."

(I agree with Mum.)

At least Dad has brought the car so I don't have to walk home with this ▬▬✂ brush sticking out of my hair. (Which is a relief.)

I can avoid people STARING at me, wondering what I've done.
I can't avoid Delia, though. When we get home, Mum and Dad are even telling Delia how FUNNY the teachers' band was.

Delia isn't listening. She's too busy looking at me and shaking her head.

She says,

"How did you do that, idiot?"

So I say, "It was an
accident – bit like your
GREEN hair.
Mum's going to help
sort it out now."

But before I get the chance to think about
what Mum is ACTUALLY going to do (CUT the
brush out), she suddenly appears with
some scissors

and does this...
SNIP! SNIP!

Then with a few more **Snip ... Snip ... SnipS...**

It's all finished. I keep my eyes closed until Mum says, "There, all gone now."

I go and take a look in the mirror to see what Mum's done.

And she's right...
It really is all gone now.

Gulp.

Delia catches me looking at my hair. I'm just waiting for her to say something HORRID as usual when she says,

"Don't worry, it will grow back ...

eventually."

Which isn't the *worst* thing she could have said, I suppose?

I go upstairs to get ready for bed, then remember to let Derek know the important news – I do a quick doodle and put it up at my window.

NEWS FLASH

THE HAIRBRUSH IS GONE

(and so is some of my hair).

Mum and Dad both come in to say goodnight.

They tell me my hair looks very cool shorter.

(I'm not so sure.)

 I think it looks a bit odd?

So I'm lying in bed, sort of going to sleep.
But I can't stop thinking about:

1. **YOU3** - so funny!

2. My CHOPPED-off hair.

If I have to sit next to Marcus (when he
stops itching and comes back to school) with
my hair like this, he'll probably just keep
making stupid jokes all the time.

Which will drive me

BONKERs.

Did you cut your hair with a knife and fork?

Hair today gone tomorrow

Then all of a sudden, I get one of MY
VERY BEST-ever ideas that comes to
me in a *FLASH.*

I ju**m**p out of bed quickly and grab
a comb.

Until my hair grows back a bit more, I could just do this?

Let's see if it works...

OH YES!

swap sides!

ANOTHER...

GENIUS IDEA

If I do say so myself...

(Thank you ... thank you.)

How to make a PAPER BANGER

1 A sheet of paper.

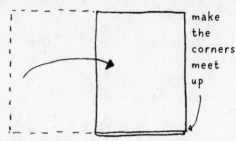

make the corners meet up

2 Fold in half.

3 Then fold in quarters.

4 Then UNFOLD the paper. There should be nice fold marks now.

5 Fold down the corner to meet the middle fold line.

6 Do the same with every corner.

7

8 Your paper should look like this.

9 Now fold the paper in half, with the flaps inside.

10 Fold the right corner to the middle.

11 Then repeat on the other side.

12 Fold the whole banger in half, hold the corners marked, then flick it down HARD.

Air catches under here to make a BANG!

BANG!

It's just as well that Joey took some other film for our video because the one that Mr Fingle helped set up didn't really work.

For obvious reasons...

This is what our video from
Mr Fingle did look like

Tom Gates' Glossary

(Which means explanations for stuff
that might sound a bit ODD.)

A4 paper — It's a paper size (BIGGER than letter size 8½ x 11).

Biscuits ≅ cookies.

Caramel wafers: 'Excellent' biscuits (cookies) ⬆ covered in chocolate with layers of caramel and wafer inside.

Chips ⇨ ≅ French fries.

CROSS = angry.

DAFT = Crazy

Dodgy = something that's a bit ODD or wrong.
Maybe slightly peculiar or not quite right. For
instance: That apple looks a bit **Dodgy.**
That monster looks

a bit dodgy. ←(worm)

Fruit chews = a candy

Garden is a YARD

Lessons = are the same as
CLASSES.

Mad = another word for crazy

 Mate = `FRIEND`

MERITS are special POINTS or STARS awarded by your teacher for excellent work.

Pudding ≡ dessert (all kinds — yum!)

 is the attendance book that the teacher would ✓ tick you off in, in the morning to make sure you're not LATE.

Rumbled! basically means

You're busted!

 Sports Kit

 is another word for TELEVISION.